Craving
OBLIVION

PART 2 OF THE OBLIVION SERIES
BY ALEXA PADGETT

ISBN-978-1-945090-33-2

Editor: Jessica Royer Ocken
Proofreading by: Charity Chimni
Cover by: Chris Philpot

For Tina.

I don't know if I would be here without your support.

Chapter 1
ELEVEN MONTHS LATER
Nash

I headed back into the house my band had rented for the weekend in San Francisco, the latest stop on our tour. Restless energy sizzled over me, as it always did, leaving me unsettled. I hated crowds and hated parties as they reminded me of Lindsay, the drugs, losing Aya.

Dammit. I had to let that go. I had to because Aya had ghosted. I still couldn't believe she'd left me.

Our album had taken longer to write and record than I'd originally planned, in large part because I was such a fucking mess when I'd arrived in Seattle last summer.

But Asher Smith had remained patient, and in time the album took shape—with a more melancholy tone for the final three songs, the last ones I'd written. We'd kicked off our tour in Seattle two months ago—just after our album's launch in February. It was an early birthday present to me. Since then, we'd worked our way through the Pacific Northwest before circling back to end our tour here. Already we were in discussions to add more dates. Asher wanted another album. Fans clamored for our songs, our merch, us. Everyone said we were the hottest new band, and we had platinum sales to back that up.

I should've been happy. Ecstatic. I'd achieved more than Brad ever had. I had complete creative control over my next EP, and we could add a month or a year or whatever we wanted to our tour—we sat right at the top of the music world.

This was where I'd wanted to be.

I just never thought it would feel so fucking hollow.

The first song I'd written for myself—the one I wrote for Aya after dropping her off in Boston while touring with Cam—remained our most popular hit, and I sang it every night. And every time, I hated what it represented. There'd been so much hope in that song, but Aya had ditched me, unwilling to hear the truth—both in the song and in my actions.

I mean, the lawyers had finally managed to get that video of Lindsay and me down, along with the many others that popped up, but they weren't able to get all the shares removed, and Holyoke students had commented on my breakup with Aya for weeks afterward.

The whole time I was in Seattle last summer, trying to get my shit together and record an album, I kept expecting Aya to return to Austin—at least to start at UT. But she didn't. And her housekeeper finally told me she'd left her cell phone at her mom's house. She deleted all her social media accounts and seemed to slide off the Earth.

Like Hugh had said: Aya was gone.

"Nash," Jax, my rhythm guitarist, called as I made it to the French doors.

"What?" I asked as I looked over my shoulder, pleased to see Steve wasn't following me.

Finally, in the last few weeks he seemed to have gotten the message that I wasn't going to talk to him or forgive him. I wouldn't even have kept him around, but that was part of the deal I'd made with Asher—that Steve would keep an eye on me.

Steve could do that, but it didn't mean I'd listen to a word he said. In fact, since losing Aya, fighting with Steve had given me a purpose—a person to hate. And I did hate him. I blamed him for letting Brad treat me so terribly, and I blamed him for sleeping with my mother. I blamed him for letting Aya walk away, too, even though that made no sense. She'd left because she wanted to.

Except…she'd left because she was hurt and humiliated. I'd just never expected Aya to believe Lindsay—*fucking Lindsay*—over me.

But Chuck had told me again and again that the photos had been damning. The social media responses from people we'd gone to school with, who'd known Aya, were merciless—many of them saying she never should have been with me in the first place, either because she was smart, or worse, because of her heritage. Both pissed me off because both were so damn wrong. Problem was, I'd never been able to get in touch with Aya to tell her that.

Her lack of trust slashed through me again, as it always did. But it also fueled my anger. She, of all people, should have known how I felt about her. So what if I couldn't use the precise words she wanted? I should have, but she *knew* me. She'd known me for years.

That's why I'd stopped trying to reach out. I finally figured maybe I didn't know her. I'd certainly been wrong about lots of other things in my life.

"Take a look at the email Hugh sent you," Jax called. "Then come back outside. I have a surprise for you."

I grunted. But I did look at the email. I nearly cracked my phone case as rage settled over me. Hugh had sent me a photo. Aya. With a guy. She stared straight ahead, but he had his hands on her. He was leaning down, whispering in her ear.

Her eyes called to me. But they were different. A shiver ran up my spine as I realized they were cold. Empty. Just like they'd been the last time I saw her, when I'd watched them drain of love and hope.

"You see it?" Jax called again after a moment. "Hugh said for me to tell you, and I quote, 'She's moved on, man.'" He appeared in the doorway, wearing swim trunks and no shirt. He was happy to show off his tanned, toned chest and abs. The girls here loved him. "I have to agree with your buddy," he continued. "You need to, too. It's been months of you dragging your ass. You never partied with us in Seattle, and you hardly ever go out with us now. We head back to Austin tomorrow, and—"

I clenched my jaw and groaned. "I'm not going back." No way in fuck I was going to live in the house where Lev had died, where I'd lost Aya, where I'd found out what giant liars my parents were.

Do you love me, Nash? I gripped my hand into a fist, gnashing my teeth. Aya had fucking dropped me like a chipped guitar pick.

"What?" I asked, turning to the sink to get a glass of water.

Jax frowned, aware I'd zoned out.

I did that often these days—fell into my own world. It had gotten me through the first month or so of the tour. But that numbness had begun to wear thin. I needed something else. No way I was ready to deal with all the emotions bubbling up.

Jax took a little step back before he held up his hands in

supplication. "I just said I get that Austin's hard for you. Still, you should let loose." He smiled. "That surprise?" He turned and looked over his shoulder toward the pool. "Nadia," he called.

A lithe, buxom redhead sidled around Jax, into the kitchen, and toward me. She wore the micro-est of bikinis, barely covering her nipples, and the thong so tiny, it left nothing to the imagination.

"Nadia wanted to get to know you." Jax smirked. "Why don't you go in the living room or upstairs where she can kiss your hurts all better?"

I set my glass of water on the counter and studied the beautiful woman in front of me. There were always beautiful women around. For the most part, they left me alone. Jax said I gave off an unapproachable vibe. I didn't care what it was as long as no one touched me.

Nadia strode forward with well-oiled hips that told me she'd walked a few runways in her life.

"How old are you?" I asked.

She fluttered her lashes as she reached forward to trace my pec through my shirt. "Old enough to know how to make you feel good," she purred.

"Not interested." I was never interested—I'd seen sex used as a weapon. Plus, the only woman I wanted was Aya.

"Let me change your mind." She tossed her hair, and I counted five freckles on her shoulder, bunched together in a cluster.

Those freckles caused me to waver toward want. And the wavering pissed me off. But Aya had moved on—I'd seen the picture with my own eyes.

Maybe I'd gone about this the wrong way. Maybe this was the

only way for me to move on, too. My mother had a new boy-friend every couple of months and said she was happier now than she'd ever been.

This wasn't about using sex as a weapon; it was about pleasure, about letting go. Having fun. I was a rock star. I was supposed to let loose. To party. Jax was always telling me. Hugh, too.

They were happy. Gratified. Relaxed. I couldn't remember the last time I felt good.

Yes, I could. The last time I was with Aya.

She'd moved on. So should I.

I slipped my arm around Nadia's waist, but every fiber of my being revolted, remembering the perfection of my time with Aya.

I stiffened as my gaze roved around the room and took in the number of semi or completely nude women. The place reeked of sex.

My stomach turned at the smell—a smell I associated with Brad. I booked it down the hall to the bathroom, where I wretched and wretched.

This attempt to move on had left me…dark. Stained. Broken.

Nadia slipped in behind me.

"Oh. I didn't realize you weren't well." She nibbled her lip. She lifted a miniscule bag at her side. "Want something to take the pain away?"

That sounded like Lindsay. I edged back, fearful of what was in there. Fear and guilt rioted inside me, and I wanted to crash my fists against my temples—anything to make the feelings stop. I needed all the feelings to disappear.

I grabbed the pill she offered and slammed it back.

Chapter 2
ONE YEAR LATER
Aya

"Aren't you going to say *anything*?" Yamir asked, running his fingers through his wavy brown hair.

It was chocolate brown—I steered clear of men with sun-kissed hair, just as I refused to date anyone with whiskey-brown eyes.

Or who were taller than six one or could sing. Or that I actually cared about.

"There's nothing to say," I replied.

I stared past him, waiting for him to run out of emotional steam and leave. I remained a few feet away on the large terrace, looking out over the sprawling traditional British garden. I wished I could transport myself to the gazebo at the far end. I needed to be alone.

I touched my wrist, after all this time, still not used to my missing malas.

I'd had nearly two years to acclimate to my life without Mum, without Nash, but nothing had seemed to level out.

"You think there's nothing to say about the fact that I want you to be more emotionally available?" Yamir snapped.

Yamir Ali, the scion of United Arab Emirates oil barons, paced and cursed, clearly not used to breaking up.

I'd dated him to appease my father and because I wanted a connection with someone. That hadn't happened, not once. I touched my wrist again, missing the bracelet's comforting weight, missing my mother. Missing Nash, in spite of myself.

I shut down the thought before I could conjure up his face. He was traveling Europe with his band, Oblivion. The name shocked me even as it felt like an insult. Nash wanted to obliterate the life he'd had? The person I'd known? *Fine.*

He'd moved on without me. *Why* couldn't I do the same? I frowned.

"Finally, an emotion," Yamir said, throwing his hands in the air.

I blinked up at him, nonplussed by his dramatics. "I have emotions. And right now, I'm annoyed." I sighed. "Look, it's been fun, but it's over."

Yamir reached forward and gripped my bare shoulders. The gown I wore tonight was held in place by a swath of material that wound close to my neck and clasped to the high panel on my chest, leaving my shoulders and upper back bare. The rose color complemented my skin and the exorbitant price tag hadn't caused me to flinch, so at the urging of Harriet, my father's wife, I'd bought her and my younger sisters' gowns, too.

"You can't mean that, Aya," Yamir protested. "I'm good for you. We could have fun in bed." He smiled, flashing his white even teeth, made even more stark against his tanned skin.

I kept my face devoid of emotion, not wanting to offend him. His kisses were…fine. But I'd never experienced anything like being held in Nash's arms. I stepped away, hugging my waist, needing to break this abominable habit of comparing every man I met to Nash Porter.

At least I hadn't had sex with him.

"This is over, Yamir," I said, my tone as cool as my interest in him. "Accept it like a gentleman."

He stared at me for a long moment, his jaw ticking, before he sneered. "You are a cold, tiny-hearted bitch." He stomped away.

I sighed, touching my elegant updo. Breaking up with men was tiresome. Life, in general, was an annoyance.

That could be, in part, because I was still in London, attending yet another party of the social season at my father's request. "*You're about to start your junior year at university, Aya. It's time for you to plan out the next stage of your life,*" he'd told me. "*Princess Diana was about your age when she married Charles.*"

The princess might have been older, but I felt ancient. I pulled my phone from my clutch, taking a moment for myself. The alert I saw there stilled my breath. My mouth formed the word *no*, but I couldn't manage to exhale.

Model and actress Carolina Syad killed in fiery crash near Milan

Oh, Nash. His mother was dead. I pressed the back of my hand to my mouth, then bolted inside and wove my way through the partygoers.

Harriet waylaid me with a soft hand to my arm. "What's wrong, dear? Yamir seemed upset."

I blinked. *Yamir? Right.* "We broke up."

Harriet sighed in that soft but disdainful way that told me she wasn't happy. "And whose fault was that?"

"Mine," I said, tone flat. "Now, if you'll excuse me, I want to go home."

She narrowed her eyes for a moment before a calculating gleam appeared. "I understand."

No, she didn't. She didn't care, either.

I needed my space. I longed to be back in Austin, in one of the apartments near UT's downtown campus, going to school and making friends with people there who I'd cherish for the rest of my life. I'd never felt grounded, settled the way I had during my time in Austin—despite how it fell apart at the end. I still wondered if I could get it back.

But I'd given up Austin, and London was my home. Here I'd been so half-hearted about friendships, so leery about getting close to someone, that I didn't have those connections I craved.

I trailed behind my stepmother. Maybe if I got my own flat near my university, I'd come to love London. There were so many things to do in the city, surely I could find my place. I needed to get out from under my father and Harriet's heavy thumbs. I closed my eyes, wishing for the warm acceptance that had cloaked me in Austin. I'd planned to be there forever. My home base.

Losing the roots I'd put down hurt. Though not as much as losing my mother or Nash.

I sighed.

Poor Nash.

His mother's death would devastate him. I needed to be there.

"I don't want you, you stupid bitch."

Even after all this time, those words rang through my head, shortening my breaths. Maybe I shouldn't go.

———

I mulled the decision through the night and the next day, even as I packed. As I moved, I realized my ability to pack and travel remained an intrinsic part of me. Perhaps I was destined for a life as a vagabond. My years-long stops in Nepal and Austin had just been minor blips.

Resolved to put my pain aside, to honor the boy I'd once loved and be there for Nash—in the event it turned out he needed me—I headed to the Eurotunnel. A restlessness filled me as I arrived in Calais, a desire to see Nash, to touch him, followed by a need to run away, to hide from the pain and shame of the last time I saw him. I hated this push-and-pull I always felt when I thought of Nash. I hated that even after all this time, he still held so much sway over my happiness.

I had booked a lovely room at La Réserve Paris, mere steps from the Champs-Élysées. I appreciated the silk-damask walls and the large suites, each with its own terrace overlooking Avenue Montaigne. Once settled in my room, having tipped the bellhop handsomely to bring my luggage to the bedroom's large closet, I stood at the floor-to-ceiling window and considered my options.

I was here, in the same city as Nash's grandfather. I assumed, based on my most recent search, that Nash's mother would be buried in the family cemetery near the Syad estate. I didn't feel as confident about my decision to come here now, but I had two days to decide whether or not to attend the funeral.

I spent both of those days waffling. Nash *might* need me, but he'd have built relationships with his bandmates by now. From the stories I'd read, Nash and Jax seemed closest, but Bridger was solid and would surely be there for him during this time of need. They'd been three for a long time, though they'd added a fourth member to the band in recent months when Jax switched from bass to rhythm guitar. All I knew was the new addition was a woman. I didn't like to think about it much beyond that.

Plus, Nash had Cam and Steve, maybe even Hugh.

I walked the streets of Paris and chewed my lip until it was raw.

In the end, I kept thinking about how much I'd missed him at *my* mother's funeral.

So when the hour arrived, I dressed in a fitted black dress from an up-and-coming American designer because I loved the understated, tucked pleats, which made my waist look even narrower and added a couple of inches to my legs. At five four, I'd never be willowy like Lindsay or Nash's mother.

Perhaps it was vain to think of my clothes right now, but I had to look my best—I had to beat back the anxiety that clawed at me on the drive to the funeral. I sighed with relief when I was able to enter without fanfare and take a seat toward the back.

I bowed my head, trying to be inconspicuous, and I startled when someone settled next to me. *Hugh.*

"He'll be glad you're here," Hugh said. "It's been a hell of a year."

I made a noncommittal sound, refusing to admit I'd cried over every new picture of Nash with another model or actress. Even when he was "between relationships" he was surrounded by beautiful women.

"He needs you, Aya."

I shook my head. "Nash needs no one."

Hugh sighed, but before he could say anything else, the mass started. I craned my neck to get a glimpse of Nash, who sat next to his ailing grandfather near the front. Tears threatened as I realized Nash would be back in this church for another service sooner rather than later.

As soon as my gaze landed on his profile, Nash stiffened. He raised his head, scanning the cavernous sanctuary until his eyes found mine. The storms I saw there brewed hotter than ever before.

Chapter 3
Nash

Aya was here? After years of missing her, *she was here*. Why? Why would she show up now after years of refusing contact?

My pulse thrummed in my neck, and I clenched my fists as adrenaline surged. The world seemed clearer, sharper—more painful.

I'd begun to stand when Pop Syad growled, "What are you doing?"

"Aya…"

"You can see the girl after we bury your mother."

The final conversation I'd had with my mom spun through my mind, making my chest ache and my palms clammy. My heart sped up as I settled back against the velvet cushion. I couldn't relax, didn't hear much of anything during the service. I'd become accustomed to retreating from pain, from any kind of feelings, really.

I squeezed my eyes tight, wishing I could go back, take back what I'd said—find a way to fix our broken relationship so it didn't end with her tears and my anger.

To appease Pop Syad, I managed to wait until the pallbearers carried my mother's coffin from the sanctuary before I charged toward the back of the church, Aya's name on my lips.

"Why are you here?" I growled even as I yanked her into my

arms. A sob built in my throat as I pressed my nose into my spot where her neck met her shoulder. I needed this, just as I needed to tell her why this ragged hurt and the guilt would never leave me.

She rose on her tiptoes, cradling my head in her slender arms. After a long moment, reality intruded, and I heard people shuffling out of their seats, some speculating about who I was hugging.

I miss you. So fucking much. But this hurts too much. How can this feel worse than burying my mother?

Before I managed to say words, I felt a hand on my arm. Aya stiffened as she stepped back.

"Who's this?" demanded Tatum, the newest member of Oblivion.

Aya's eyes shuttered, and I watched, horrified, as the girl I'd known slid behind a façade of etiquette. "Aya Aldringham," she began politely. "Nash and I—"

Tatum smirked. "Right. The infamous ex. I'm impressed you showed up today. Says a lot about your ability to move on."

I stepped in front of Tatum, a low growl in my chest. "Tatum's our bassist."

Aya dropped her gaze to where Tatum had laid her hand on my biceps, her fingers spread wide to cover as much of my black suitcoat as possible.

Then Pop Syad joined us, jamming his walker between Tatum and Aya. "Aya, my girl. I've missed you."

Tatum winced as Pop Syad stepped on her toes. Bridger and Jax came to flank my sides, both of them glaring at Tatum, who now stared fixedly at a spot on the cathedral's farthest wall, her jaw locked.

Aya shook her head at Pop Syad's murmured words. "I couldn't. This…" The old Aya rose into her eyes, and her face warmed as she took Pop's hand in hers. She spoke in French, keeping her gaze on him. Then, before I realized her intent, she'd turned and melted into the crowd exiting through the massive wooden doors.

I stepped toward her, but Pop Syad angled in front of me. "Don't embarrass her further," he said, turning his glare toward Tatum. "And you…" He curled his lip, disgust evident in his tone and expression, his accent heavier than usual. "You are not invited into my home."

Tatum drew in a sharp breath as Pop Syad moved forward, his bodyguards parting the flow of mourners and paparazzi.

I started after him, but Tatum gripped my suitcoat again. "What do you want?" I snapped.

"Why was she here?" Tatum whined.

"I couldn't say."

Hugh stepped forward. "She came to see you. Check in. Make sure you're all right, what with your mom's death and all." His eyes narrowed. "You know, all those things you should have done for her when her mom died."

Bridger gaped. "You left the girl to deal with her mom's death alone? Fuck, Nash, that's some cold shit."

I gritted my teeth. "Not because I wanted to," I said. "I was in the hospital."

"Aya didn't know that," Hugh noted helpfully.

I pulled back. "Does she know now? What Lindsay did?"

He shrugged. "She wasn't in a good place, and she left with

her dad right after the funeral. I have no idea if she heard any-thing I told her when I visited her. She was…I've never seen her like that. She was wrecked."

"Who cares?" Tatum groaned. "Why are we still talking about the snooty bitch?"

Hugh rounded on her, his glare hotter than the midday sun.

But I spoke first. "Jax, Bridge, would you take Tatum back to the hotel? I need to spend the afternoon with my grandfather."

"Aw, c'mon, Nash," Tatum said. "Don't be sad. We'll hit a club, show these Frenchies how to part-ay!" She bounced up and down, reminding me of Lindsay Herrington-Smythe that night.

Hugh shuffled back, grimacing. Clearly, he was thinking the same thing.

I raised my eyebrows at Jax and Bridger, who steered Tatum out of the cathedral.

"Is Aya even studying engineering?" I asked.

Hugh shrugged. "She cut me out of her life, too."

I shook my head. "That doesn't make any sense."

Hugh shoved his hands into his suit pockets. He wore suits often now that he was completing his MBA. He'd spent the first two summers of college working for Asher's record label, but last summer he'd been in Boston with one of the premier private equity firms, buying and breaking up companies. I'd thought, for a while, that he'd be my manager once he graduated, but he'd refused my overtures about the time I quit listening to Asher's advice.

I barely tolerated Cam's continued attempts to connect these days. I didn't like either of my idols, my mentors, to see how deep I'd sunk into the rock-and-roll lifestyle.

"I was mad for a long time," Hugh said with a shrug. "But then I saw the video again. Last year—remember when it hit the media sites?"

I grunted, annoyed. That joyride had come alongside a night I couldn't really remember—I'd been so high that the show nearly didn't happen. The internet had dug up the video of me at Hugh's birthday party and headlines compared my drug problem with my mother's. My mom. The weight of her death settled over me. *Dammit.* I wanted Aya. I wondered if she still had the ability to make things better for me.

"I'm not an addict," I told him.

Hugh leveled me with a look. "As I was saying—about *Aya.* I watched the video. It's really bad, Nash. The way Lindsay spins it…if I hadn't been there for the whole thing, I would think you were dumping Aya, too."

I began walking toward the doors. "No way. And I'm seriously pissed she'd think that. Still pissed."

Aya had noted my reaction when I first saw her during the service, and she'd dropped her gaze. And then Tatum had acted all possessive. But…I wasn't in the wrong on this. Aya left *me.* I shoved open the doors to the church.

"You can ride with me," Hugh said as I stared at the nearly empty parking lot.

Right. I'd come over with my grandfather. I shook my head. I needed a drink. Or a hit. Something to ease the tension headache I had brewing.

I settled into the back seat next to Hugh and closed my eyes, thankful for a moment with an old friend who didn't want more from me than my company. From the moment Oblivion's first album had dropped and flown up the charts, slamming into platinum sales within a couple of weeks and garnering us a best new artist and best album Grammy, I'd been bombarded with attention.

"Here." Hugh thrust his phone in my hand.

I cracked open one eye. "I've seen it." I moved to end it, but I couldn't. Because Hugh was right—from this angle, I looked like I was making out with Lindsay's tits. Her triumphant smile and ugly words embodied the new girlfriend preening before the sad ex.

It ended with the fool videographer cackling as Aya slid past, her shoulders hunched in, tears brimming in her eyes.

Steve was in the front seat next to Hugh's driver. He turned as I looked up.

"You've seen this?" I asked him. It was one of the first times I'd addressed him in months.

He nodded.

My hands twitched as nervous energy filled me. "Did you know she was going to leave?"

"No."

"Is she going to school at least?"

He cleared his throat. "Yes. She's attending Imperial College in London."

"Is that a good school?"

He shrugged. "It's the best one in the area, I believe."

I shoved my fingers through my hair, hating the idea of her losing out on any education and associated opportunities because of a mean girl's prank in high school.

"Aya thought you were with Tatum," Hugh said as I returned

his phone. "That's what she said to your grandfather—that she hadn't meant to cause a problem with your girlfriend."

My stomach rolled. "She deserved that after ditching me like she did. Hurts to have your lo—someone you care about flaunt a new significant other."

"Aya never flaunted a boyfriend," Hugh said. "There was one pic of her with that dude, and I regret sending it to you. She clearly cared enough today to set aside your past, and you have to admit that video looks bad, like you wanted to fuck Lindsay."

I clenched my jaw. "I didn't do anything wrong. I was drugged! Aya ghosted me before I even got out of the hospital."

Hugh shook his head. "You had to see the hurt on her face when Tatum slithered all over you today."

"I saw it," I muttered, trying to ignore the regret that wanted to flood my chest.

Chapter 4
Aya

I sighed, touching my elegant updo as Benton blubbered. Why had I thought dating a man would help me feel better about my encounter with Nash?

Damn him! More than a month later, and I still couldn't stop rehashing his mother's funeral. Not ideal.

I preferred the long, grueling hours in the physics lab— redoing a problem for the umpteenth time to double check my results—to listening to a man whining. But these tense and uncomfortable moments always ended the same way.

I'd hoped, briefly, that Benton would be *the one*. However, he'd proven more emotional and moodier than Yamir, and less interesting, too.

"No wonder they call you Ice Queen," Benton said as he flounced off.

I lifted my glass of champagne and sipped as I stared out into the beautiful symmetry of the English garden.

These events bored me. This wasn't the way I'd seen my life unfolding, but I didn't have the fight in me to blaze a new path anymore. I just needed to forge some semblance of roots and permanence out of what I had available. At least I had my career, which gave me purpose. And my flat here in London. Friends had proved elusive, to say nothing of a relationship worth sustaining, but my goal hadn't wavered. Since we'd left Nepal and my mother decided to stop traveling, I'd wanted nothing more than a home.

And as always, that made me think of Austin.

I clenched my fists, trying to stymie the deep ache that carved out my middle. I missed my mother, my friends, my home. I missed my life.

"Are you all right?"

I turned, trying to extinguish the annoyance that lit me up at the intrusion. "Fine, thank you," I said. "And you?"

A faint smile teased around his lips. He stepped forward, into the light, and I noted his wheat-blond hair and pale blue eyes. His features were straight, if a bit dull, and he was tall but not so tall so as to tower over me—to make me feel dainty, petite. Feminine.

"Oh, I'm well, Miss Aldringham. But your tete-a-tete with Benton seemed...heated." He smirked at the word choice, no doubt having heard Benton call me Ice Queen.

My scowl deepened as his gaze moved to my chest before rising back up toward my eyes in a leisurely pass. My gown was demure with a hint of sexiness, as befitted my status—at least according to my father.

"I'm not familiar with you," I said, my tone cool. "Perhaps you'd be so kind as to introduce yourself?"

His smile turned wicked. "Alistair Seymour. Your father assured me I was known to you."

I raised an eyebrow. "Whatever my father told you is based on his belief that I actually listen to what he says, which I can assure you, I do not."

Alistair laughed. He held out his hand, and I allowed him

to take mine by the fingers before flipping it over and pressing a soft, warm kiss to the middle of my palm.

I quashed my initial reaction to withdraw my hand, knowing he hoped to get a rise out of me. "Are you a peer, then, Alistair Seymour?"

"I am in line to be an earl, and you, my dear, are a highly sought commodity. Tell me, what was it about Benton that turned you off so completely?"

I leaned in a little and fluttered my lashes. "His innate confidence that any woman should fall at his feet." With that I swept around Alistair, as one can only do when dressed for these large social gatherings.

I wanted to go home, take off my makeup, remove the pins from my hair, and throw this gown on the floor. I wanted to flop on my bed in a pair of sweats. I was so over the constant soirees and parties. "*Necessary evils, my dear,*" my father told me if I complained. *"How else do we gain access to the peerage?"*

He believed that. But lately, I'd also noticed that my trust fund balance dipped thanks mostly to *his* expenditures—more than the gowns or even the school fees for my sisters or my tuition. I wondered if my father kept me around to marry me off or to use me as his personal savings account.

After my breakdown, which had corresponded to a photo of Nash with a pretty blond model soon after I'd come to England, I hadn't cared a fig about my inheritance. I'd focused solely on gaining access to the engineering program at Imperial College, refusing to take a gap year or attend a less well-regarded university. I was going to be an engineer. And a damn fine one.

No matter what else happened, I would have my work. I could create a life for myself entirely within that world, if needed.

Consequently, I hadn't bothered to look at my bank statements until this past month when I'd managed to snag the mail off the bureau in the main hall of the country estate…and realized my father was spending fifteen thousand pounds or more *each month*.

That had sped up my decision to get my own flat, and since then, I'd removed Father from my bank accounts. He had railed against both those decisions before turning darkly silent.

"How about we head back inside, and I can catch you up on my most recent communique with your father?" Alistair asked.

I pressed my fingertips to my forehead. "I've a bit of a headache. Another time, perhaps?" I smiled to ease the rejection. I really did have a headache, no doubt caused by the stress of my interactions with Benton and the cursed hairpins.

"Then I shall take you home." Alistair smiled down at me, eyes twinkling. "I only came tonight as a favor to a friend."

I suppressed the urge to snort, knowing it wasn't done in high society. "Look, Lord…?" I raised my eyebrows.

"Alistair is fine."

I swallowed, taken aback by his warmth and lack of typical decorum.

"Well, Alistair. As you noted, I've recently removed myself from a rather horrid relationship and have no interest in starting another."

"Who said anything about a relationship?" Alistair took my hand and hooked it around his arm, patting my fingers to keep them on the crease of his elbow.

We entered through the terrace doors, and I felt Benton's hot gaze burning into mine. My headache pounded against my skull as I tried to figure out Alistair's angle.

"Lord Seymour."

I froze as Alistair turned me toward the voice I'd never forget, and yet I still ended up staring into the wide, hurt eyes of Lindsay Herrington-Smythe, the girl Nash had been with the night my future ended.

Chapter 5
Nash

The pounding beat rushed through me. *Living* the music provided a high that hearing it in my head never had. I let it take me, the hum of the chords and the scream of the fans filling me up. I glanced over at Bridger, who pounded on the drums, his muscles corded, sweat dripping down his long nose as we built to a frantic crescendo. I pulled my guitar up and brought it down as Bridger slammed his drumsticks into the snare at his knees.

For a moment, all I heard was my own breathing. Bridger's grin widened, his eyes glazed with the same adrenaline that pumped through me. Then, all the sound rushed back in—screams and air horns, Jax whooping next to me. I turned enough to see him bouncing up and down, his arms over his head like he'd won an Olympic gold medal.

The rush built, carrying me higher. I loved this feeling, wanted to stay here, floating in it forever. *This* was what performing was about.

A woman leaped onto the stage, screaming my name. Her hair was dark, an inky black against the lights. Her body small and curvy. For a moment, everything in me froze. *Aya.*

Security moved to intercept the woman, but not before I caught a glimpse of her face. Her eyes were brown, her nose too big. Her lips too thin.

Definitely not Aya.

I hadn't seen her since my mother's funeral six weeks ago. I'd tried to find her afterward, but she'd checked out of her hotel in Paris by the time I got there. Pop Syad had raked me hard for my treatment of her, but I'd ignored him and left early the next morning.

Now I wished I hadn't. Most of my family was gone.

I'd been back in Paris for Pop's funeral last week. I'd hoped Aya might attend. She hadn't.

Don't think about that. Get through this song. Get through the next. You'll be off stage soon. Just hold it together.

"I love you," the woman screamed.

I smirked as I leaned into the microphone, giving it a soft caress, much like I had Aya's soft belly.

"I love you, too. All of you," I purred. Her screaming stopped. "And that's why we're going to play one more song." I nodded to Bridger who knocked his sticks together, finding his beat.

Security dragged the now-sobbing woman offstage as I ripped through the chords, willing the music to take me back to that place—the one where I didn't have to feel anything other than this high.

Jax threw his arms around me, pulling me tight to his side as we headed toward the hotel suite we'd booked for the after party. *Where are we?* Shit, I didn't remember. This tour had been relentless. I glanced up at a billboard of the local hockey team. *Ah! Boston. Right.* Sweat and smoke, both tobacco and pot, clung to my clothes, my hair. My arms and legs shook as the last vestiges of adrenaline seeped from my body. Exhaustion filtered into my brain.

"You're going to join us tonight, right?" Tatum asked. Her voice, always a bit raspy, now held the husky quality of lust. She offered me a hint of a smile. She'd been smart enough not to touch me since she'd made it seem like we were a couple the day of my mother's funeral.

I hadn't needed to read her the riot act; by the time I'd returned to the hotel, both Bridger and Jax had informed her that if she behaved like that again, she'd be out of the band.

I shook my head.

Her bright eyes, filled with hope and passion, dimmed. Her lush mouth melted into disappointment as she walked away.

Jax tossed back his sweat-soaked bangs. "She still refuses to let go of the fantasy that you're going to get really hot for her."

"I'm not. Ever."

"Might be time to get rid of her, then," Jax said. "And you— you need to deal with your shit because your head is all over the place. You need to let off some steam. Fuck it out, man."

That was Jax's answer for everything, the one I'd tried back in San Francisco. I knew it didn't work.

I shook my head. He didn't know what had gone down that night with the model, and I didn't plan to tell him. Embarrassment crept up my neck, and just the *idea* of cracking like that again caused any desire I might have had for a woman to wane.

Steve moved to my side—a silent, annoying, yet welcome presence. I still hated him—hated him just as much as I leaned on him. It was codependent and messed up, but he was the closest thing I had to a father.

Hell, he could *be* my father.

"Why don't you go to the party?" Steve said.

Bridger clasped my shoulders from behind before he bounced ahead, yelling, "Let's part-ay!"

I cringed, hating those words. *Fucking Lindsay.*

I turned away from Steve, ignoring his scowl. Then I opened the door to my suite and stopped cold.

"Cam?" I said, blinking hard.

Steve glanced into the suite, a look of relief sweeping over his face, before he shut the door, offering me more privacy than I typically had. I appreciated the gesture. I should probably tell him that.

"Good to see you, son," Cam said. He pulled a Werther's from his pocket and slipped the candy between his lips. "Sorry I missed your mama's funeral—and your Pop's too. You've had a hell of a run."

"Don't worry about that." I waved my hand. "You've had your own shit going on."

"True, but you'll always be important to me."

"I thought you were touring farther south."

Cam scratched his cheek. "Manhattan. Closest we've been in over a year."

I dropped my gaze. I hadn't been back to Austin since Aya... I shut that thought down.

"So I decided to pay you a visit."

"I've been busy," I said, heat creeping up my neck. Cam was busy too, but he made time for me. I hadn't returned the favor. I didn't want him to see me high or drunk, not after he and Asher had tried so hard to keep me clean and straight.

They shouldn't have bothered.

"I got hitched," he said. "Sent you an invite, but I guess you never got it."

My breath left me in a rush. *Cam? Married?* I'd seen some reports about him and a pretty blonde, but marriage? I swallowed hard, hoping for his sake that he'd made the right choice.

"No, I... No, I wouldn't have missed that."

Unless I had. My mind spun out a lot these days. Maybe I'd forgotten. Didn't that make me a shit person? I swallowed, wishing it was a drink. Whiskey would go down nice and smooth right about now.

"Congratulations," I said.

He smiled. "Thanks. You're gonna love her—Jenna. She builds guitars. Beautiful, perfect instruments."

"Great." I moved forward and settled on the sofa.

Cam's smile widened, and contentment radiated off of him. He'd been so dead-set against love. My stomach soured as I realized he'd let go of his past.

Damn, I *really* needed a drink.

"Why are you here?" I asked.

His eyes twinkled. "To tell you about the love of my life."

I failed to suppress my shiver of revulsion at the word *love.* Cam would pay for allowing himself to have that damned emotion. He'd probably sink into the same cycle of douchery Brad had. I didn't want that for him.

I raised an eyebrow.

He sighed. "Fine. Are you still not willing to talk to your girl? It's been years. I heard *she* made your mama's funeral."

I rose, legs wobbly. The one topic even more off-limits than Aya was my mother. Guilt clawed its way up my chest. "Cam, you have been the single person in my life I could count on, but right now, I need you to leave."

He didn't move. "Heard tell you refused to stay for the reading of your grandfather's will."

"I heard the important bits from Pop's assistant, Cynthia."

"Ah, yeah, she called me. Let me know about how Aya fit into your grandfather's plans—"

"I don't care." I slashed through the air with my hand. Guilt, disappointment, and helplessness swirled through me. "Not my business anymore."

"Well, I sent her some tickets to your show over there this summer," Cam informed me. "Thought maybe the two of you could catch up, clear the air—"

At that, I walked out of the room. I closed the bedroom door, locked it, and leaned back against it, shaking. No way I was going to listen to Cam if he brought up that night.

I snagged the bottle of vodka from my suitcase as I headed into the bathroom and turned on the shower.

Sometime later I woke up on the shower floor. I pulled my stiff, aching limbs from the tiles and flipped off the water. I staggered out of the stall, teeth chattering as I dried off and managed to make my way to the bed, my entire body shaking.

The clock read four am. I'd been in the shower for three hours.

As I lay under the blankets, my body wracked with spasms,

my mind, sluggish from the vodka, finally latched onto Cam's words. *Pop Syad's will has something to do with Aya.*

I shoved thoughts of her, of the hurt in her violet eyes, out of my mind. Wouldn't do any good to dwell on her. Too much time had passed. She was the one in the wrong anyway.

But what had the cagey old bastard tried to push on me from the grave?

SIX MONTHS LATER
Aya

I stared down at the tickets, caressing Nash's name. My fingertips tingled as the hired car slid to a stop in front of the venue. I studied the façade of London's most enormous outdoor stadium. Typically used for soccer matches, this place booked few musicians because it was no small feat to fill two hundred thousand seats.

Well, the seat next to me would be open. I still didn't have a friend I felt I could ask to the concert. I'd have to share my secrets and explain my past with the man recently touted as one of the sexiest alive. Nash's face was on the cover of the magazine that proclaimed him such.

I stepped out and took a breath as Nash's success sank into my bones. I smiled even as I pressed my back against the car, ready to flee. Though the tickets had come from Cam, Nash *might* have invited me. He might even want to apologize. Would I let him?

Did it matter now, after all these years?

"I don't want you, you stupid bitch."

I cringed as, on cue, his words roared through my head. I closed my eyes as I remembered the vicious smirks on my fellow students' faces.

I rolled my shoulders back and lifted my chin, finally stepping away from the car. He couldn't hurt me. Not anymore. I wouldn't let him.

My phone rang. "Hello, lovely Aya," Alistair began, just as

he had every other time he'd called in the past six months. He rang me multiple times each week, wooing me with kind words. Seducing me with his wit.

I was cracking. I just wanted to feel…something. And with Alistair, I did. I liked that he bent to my will, that he remained uncertain of my mood, of whether I would agree to his requests for a date.

Would I?

"Hi," I said.

"Where are you? I thought perhaps I could pick you up this evening and take you to dinner. Somewhere quiet."

His accent remained crisp, his words direct. He seemed more confident than normal.

I smiled at his new approach. Oh, I liked being chased. It made me feel bold, beautiful. Wanted. So unlike the broken girl who'd slunk from Hugh's house, head bowed so people wouldn't see my tears.

And with Alistair, I was building something: those roots I'd always wanted. If I settled here, I'd be able to find a position at one of the firms in London. The job might not be on par with something at NASA or the Jet Propulsion Laboratory, but I'd get to build satellites and other important equipment. My work would matter. And I'd have Alistair. He'd be my friend, perhaps, and soon, my lover.

"I'm out this evening, but maybe…"

I stared up at the huge banner of Nash. His sun-kissed hair looked damp, his eyes stormy and dark, and the faintest hint of his dimple flashed at his cheek. My stomach warmed.

"Soon," Alistair said. "I've given you the space you needed, Aya. I want to date you. And I think you want to say yes."

"Call me tomorrow?" I asked. Nash was my past. I'd put him there tonight. For good.

"My pleasure," Alistair replied.

I shoved the phone into the back pocket of my jeans, and my heels clicked as I walked into the stadium.

***

Truly, there was nothing in the world like a rock concert—fans pressed close, bodies thrumming with excitement, the flash of lights, the roar of pyrotechnics, the full-throated screams from women and the deeper bellows from men. This was primal. Sexy.

I pressed my thighs together, trying to ignore the pulsing in my core as Nash sang about long, hot nights in tangled sheets. The images he evoked were those of us, together. Young and tender and curious. I pressed my palms to my belly. Those were the words *my* Nash, my love, had written and now sang.

As the last note faded, a harsher, rougher beat replaced it. The band moved on to a song from the new album—the one that had dropped a few weeks before. These songs were edgier, the guitar licks almost a battle for supremacy. Discord warred in my chest with each thrum. Nash threw his head back and yelled, a guttural sound of fury.

I hated it.

When the third woman rushed the stage, my stomach rolled so hard I nearly vomited. Nash winked at her, causing her to swoon as the security guards dragged her off. When his bassist sidled up next to him, pressing her breasts into his arm, sliding her body up and down his leg in a casual simulation of sex, I squeezed my eyes shut.

I didn't open them again until the crowd roared as the band handed off their guitars and began to drift off the stage.

They'd move to the encore now.

What would they play?

Suddenly, I didn't care.

I didn't want to be here, to witness more sensual interaction between Nash and Tatum or the crowd. This, tonight, had tainted the last of the sweet memories I had of him, of us. Tears pressed behind my eyes as I shoved through the crowd.

I ended up nose-to-chest with Steve.

He smiled down at me. "I'm glad you came," he yelled. "Nash will be thrilled."

"I'm leaving," I said. "I don't want to see him."

He frowned, confusion in his eyes. We both turned to watch as Nash returned to the stage. The bass player pulled his head down, and he wrapped his arm around her waist. My chest ached. I whirled away.

"Aya," Steve called.

I dashed at the damn tears. What had I been thinking?

Nash Porter still owned my heart. No matter how much time had passed. And each time I came into his orbit, all he did was break more of it.

Chapter 7
Nash

I pushed through the door of the coffee shop, trying to ignore the pounding in my head. I'd performed most of Oblivion's brand-new third album, along with some of the classics from the first two, to a huge crowd at Wembley Stadium last night, the second of two back-to-back concerts in a jam-packed summer tour. Despite this, I didn't have the luxury of sleeping the day away as the rest of my band did. Today, instead of nursing the hangover that lurked behind my eyes, my responsibilities to the Syad empire called. They weighed me down, actually, and I barely managed to push back a groan of defeat.

At least my bandmates had known better than to drag me to the after-party. I preferred to do my unwinding separately and with a bottle of whatever liquor I could get my hands on. I felt like crap, but I knew it would've been worse with them.

I had to make more decisions about Pop's businesses—the ones he hadn't divested of prior to his death, which was a dizzying array of companies. Today, I'd meet with three separate boards of directors, none of whom were excited to talk to a twenty-two-year-old without a degree but with more money than any of them would ever accumulate.

I settled into line with Steve trailing a step behind me, as he always did, along with the other two men who now made up my service detail. Apparently, as one of the richest men in the world, I was considered a potential target for ransom or some stupid shit.

Honestly, I thought it more likely a rabid fan would jump out and try to wrestle me to the ground than I become the central figure in an abduction plot. But what the hell did I know?

I still mostly refused to talk to Steve, and I refused to consider our potential blood relationship. When Pop Syad had asked me to have a buccal swab a few years ago, when all the shit went down, I'd declined. That would've made the connection too real. Still, whether I liked it or not, he was something of a lifeline— more so since my mom and Pop Syad were gone.

I fiddled with my cufflinks, disliking my suit. Not only did I have to go to meetings today, but I had to do it dressed like a Wall Street douche.

Still, even in this outfit, I couldn't imagine needing a team of security on a quiet street in Kensington, but I'm sure John Lennon wasn't expecting a gunshot to the chest that nice day in New York, either. So I'd let Steve worry about that. I had other things on my mind—like the fact that I'd nearly managed to see Aya last night.

I'd sent Steve out to find her, but she'd rejected his invitation to come backstage. Tatum had waylaid me with a kiss—and I'd had to play along for the crowd's sake. Steve said Aya had slipped away after that. Before I could talk to her. At least I knew she was in London.

That was important to me in a way it hadn't been for a long time. Somewhere in the last few months, seeing Cam settled into married bliss, I'd begun to question my theory about love. I'd decided Aya and I *had* to talk about that night—what really happened—because it wasn't going away, and whatever we were to each other now, she remained a formative part of my life. I wasn't sure how to cut her loose, or if I really wanted to.

Hugh had made his point when he'd showed me the video again after my mother's funeral, though even then I'd refused to acknowledge how badly I'd appeared to behave. It wasn't until I actually met Cam's wife, saw how perfect they were for each other, that I realized how much I missed having Aya in my life. Jenna was a hot mess of anxiety at times, but she and Cam loved deeply, to the soul. Cam protected her, but she supported him just as much—quietly, from the wings.

Like Aya used to do for me.

I missed Aya. I missed our closeness, knowing someone cared that much for me—like Jenna did for Cam. I was devastated that I'd lost her. That's why I shrugged everyone off. That's why I took my next drink of whiskey.

But I didn't get to see Aya, to tell her any of that, likely thanks to Tatum. Oblivion's bassist sat officially at the top of my shit list, and no amount of pleading or pouting would change that. Her constant touching, the screams, the need to answer another round of her inane questions—it all grated my nerves.

As Cam had tried to tell me years ago, touring wasn't the flashy adrenaline high I'd expected. This was work—a constant grind. But the alternative was to stay in the condo in Austin and brood. I'd gotten really damn good at that and couldn't stand to do anymore.

So, I'd recorded another album and hit the road again. This was the life I knew, and the life I now realized my mother had found more comfortable than staying close to home. To me.

As I continued to wait, I turned and shook the damp condensation from my suit coat. Then, I straightened as a teasing, tantalizing scent reached my nose. *No way.* But even as I thought it, my gaze swept the room and…my breath caught. *There.* Aya.

For the first time in years, George Harrison's "Something" spun through my mind, soothing me.

She stood in front of me in the line at the coffee shop, about three people from the counter. She wore a lightweight, pale rose coat that fit her closely, showing off her slender waist. She stood with her shoulders back, more regal than I'd ever seen her. She seemed aloof, disinterested in her surroundings.

Based on her clothing, she appeared to be preparing for life as a debutante. My chest ached as I considered the brilliant mind behind those stunning eyes, forced to discuss trivialities and weather.

At that moment, she raised her head, nostrils quivering, as if she, too, had realized I was close. Her gaze slid toward me, unerring, and the smack of connection hit me hard, nearly robbing me of my balance.

But then, instead of the delight her violet gaze had once exuded, she shut down. I watched any interest fade from her already-neutral face as she turned away.

No. That wasn't my Aya. She wouldn't…

"I don't want you."

"You stupid bitch."

The words I'd said years ago came back to me—the ones she'd thought were directed toward her—and my world shifted. The hurt behind the tears in her eyes replayed in my mind.

Hugh had been right: she *still* thought I'd said those things *to* her.

I straightened my spine as I slid my hand into my pocket and fingered the malas beads I carried there. This was my chance.

Her shoulders stiffened as I left the line and came closer. I could see the tension work its way up into her jaw. As she placed her order, her soft voice requesting a large London fog, I hovered nearby, which was beginning to cause a stir, thanks to my entourage. Aya ignored me, though the rest of the customers craned their necks and pulled out their phones.

Heat rushed to my face as I realized how stupid I'd been, thinking I could simply walk up to her—as if everyone staring in the coffee shop and those terrible words wouldn't sit between us. Before she could offer her card, I laid a fifty-pound note on the counter.

"Is there a place I might speak to her, privately?" I asked the barista, keeping my voice low. "And could you bring her drink to her there once it's ready?"

I felt Aya stiffen next to me, and some banker-looking type in a bespoke suit behind me chuffed in displeasure. The thirty-something barista eyed me with adoration, even as she pocketed the note and nodded. "This way."

I touched Aya's elbow, but she jerked from my grasp, shooting me an angry glare, though she did walk with a regal sedateness toward a small side door the barista had opened. It was a well-lit storage closet, not much bigger than one of those red phone booths that still dotted London's central city.

Aya stepped in, arms crossed now as if to protect herself from me—or to hold her emotions in. I decided it was the latter when she whirled to face me, her face a mask of anger and defiance. The door clicked shut behind me, and she drew herself upward.

"I saw you last night," she said. "Congratulations on achieving your goal."

I'd wanted to write the perfect song. I'd gotten close, and it had changed my life. I shoved my hands in my pockets. "I don't want to talk about the concert."

"What *do* you want?" she asked. Her chin tipped upward in defiance, and her eyes shot sparks.

So, she wasn't as cool—as unaffected—as she pretended to be, and she didn't like my response.

"I'm sorry—"

"I don't care to hear an apology," she replied. Her accent was stronger, almost sharp.

Sadness drifted through me. I'd done this to her, to us. "Well, I'm still terribly sorry for—"

"I have an interview, and I don't wish to be late."

I swallowed hard. I'd known I'd hurt her, but I'd never seen Aya like this. So brittle. Impossible to reach.

"You promised you'd always be there for me," I said.

She whipped around, eyes blazing, lip pulled back in a sneer. "Do not ever—*ever*—talk to me about promises." She seemed to fade into herself a little. Her lower lip trembled. "You broke every one you made to me. Now, I need to go."

"Aya…" Her name was a plea.

"What? What, Nash?"

"I've missed you."

She turned to face me, a hard smile on her lips. "Yes, the fucking was quite good between us."

I winced.

"Is that what you want? A little replay? For…old time's sake?"

She threaded her arms around my neck and molded her body to mine. My hands fell to her waist, and I groaned at how good she felt against me.

I missed this connection. I'd missed her. I whispered her name.

She stiffened. "No," she whispered.

"What?"

Her breath came in ragged gusts, and she kept muttering *no*. She bolted to the door.

She looked back over her shoulder, eyes wet and wild as she struggled with the doorknob. "No. Don't. Don't touch me. Don't…"

My confusion began to shift to worry. "What's wrong?"

"Wrong?" Her laugh had a hysterical tinge. "I thought I could embarrass you like you did me. Instead, I just want you to h-hold me." Her shoulders slumped, and she sobbed. "After all this time, and as if I wasn't messed up enough already."

My pulse pounded as I tried to figure out what to do—how to fix this. I shoved my hands into my pockets and remembered the malas. I clutched them for a moment before I drew my hand out and opened it, palm up. "Maybe these will help."

Her angry gaze slid down to my hand, and her lip quivered. She reached forward before pulling her hand back, fingers trembling.

"I took them—the night I went back to your house," I confessed. "I just wanted to feel close to you…"

My words died as her face fell, and grief etched deep into her skin. "I thought I'd lost them." Her breathing grew more rapid. Tears dripped down her cheek. She looked…devastated. "*How could you?*"

The accusation in her words left me reeling. The pain in her eyes left my chest sliced open.

"I…"

Now her whole jaw trembled. She clamped it shut and reached forward, snatching the malas from my hand. The bracelet caught on my cufflink, and the thread within it gave, spilling the beads to the floor.

Aya made a desperate sound, dropping downward, hands racing to collect the tumbling red spheres. I dropped to my knees to help her.

"Haven't you ruined my life enough?" she cried. A sob overtook her. "You womanizing asshole!" She looked up into my eyes, and all the betrayal, all the pain flared.

She hadn't moved on at all. I hadn't realized. Not until this moment.

I'd cracked something fundamental inside her. She wasn't the girl I knew. She'd been altered.

Because of me.

"Aya."

I reached forward but she flinched back, her mouth puckered. "I hate you," she whispered.

I shook my head, needing her to renounce those words, but she was up on her feet, darting around me and out the door before I managed to heave a breath.

I stared down at the garnet beads still littering the floor, tears in my eyes.

Slowly, methodically, I gathered them, but I was missing one. Finally, after moving items and nearly ripping my jacket, I gave up. I shoved the beads into my pocket, hating the way they jangled there, untethered—like me.

When I opened the door, Steve stood outside, concern etched across his face as I dusted off my knees. He reached forward and brushed something from my shoulder—dirt, no doubt, from where I'd slithered under the metal shelving, searching for the last of the garnets.

"Let's go," I said.

He led me out a back door, and I returned to the sidewalk feeling wooden, my heart as broken as Aya's eyes.

———

That night, after meetings I couldn't remember, I shut the door to my bedroom at the London estate I'd inherited from Pop Syad. I'd refused to allow my bandmates to stay here while we were playing in town, not wanting them to trash the place. So at least I only had to escape Steve.

I'd picked out a bottle of liquor on my way up. Whistlepig whiskey. It was expensive—it had to be if Pop Syad had purchased it. I spent the next hour reliving this morning's conversation with Aya and downing the bottle.

"I hate you."

Such soft words, barely spoken. Yet they'd had such impact.

"I hate you."

I believed her. Once she'd loved me, fiercely. I realized that now—I'd been coming to that realization for a while. She would have done *anything* for me. But she believed I'd broken my promise. It didn't matter that I'd thought she'd broken hers.

I should have known better. To Aya, promises meant everything.

I'd failed her, thanks to my fear. Sure, Lindsay's stunt had hurt us. But I'd broken Aya because I'd set her up for that moment with my refusal to fully give her what she'd needed: my love. My assurance. My trust.

"I hate you."

After a few more swallows, I found a place where I didn't see the anger and hurt in her eyes as clearly and her words, "*I hate you,*" didn't burn straight down to my soul.

And I liked it, so I stayed there, after a while letting Steve's presence drift around me. Sure, I saw his worry, but I didn't care. I only *thought* I'd had something to escape from before. Now oblivion was the only way to cope with the pain of self-loathing, of so much wasted time and nothing but more ahead. Remaining removed, untouchable, meant I didn't have to feel.

Chapter 8
Nash

Another concert, another night, a different continent. Not much had changed since we'd launched that first West Coast tour, hot on the heels of our debut album. Except *everything* had changed in the month since I'd talked to Aya in that coffee shop. It had gotten so very much worse.

I lifted my arms, beaming out into the crowd, giving them what they wanted: me.

"Love you, Vegas!"

I hated everything about this. I remembered Asher's words on Cam's bus all those years ago, about how touring could destroy relationships. I hadn't understood then.

The screaming continued, grating on my nerves. I turned and glared at Samson, my stage manager. He spoke into the headset, and the lights blinked off. I dropped my mic, too eager to leave the stage to care about putting it back into the stand. I walked offstage.

"Great show!" Jax said, slapping me on the back, his grin wide. My muscles bunched.

"Yeah, man." Bridger's grin was so wide, I could see his crooked canine. His shaggy ginger mop appeared darker, nearly brown, thanks to the sweat from exertion on his drums. "Woo! Let's do another encore."

He might've been five years older than me and a damn fine musician, but right now he was a pain in my ass. I growled. I needed a drink—no, the bottle, especially if I was going to have to deal with Bridger's enthusiasm.

Tatum glared at me as I stomped past them, heading toward my dressing room. I had a bottle of bourbon, and I planned to empty a bunch of it.

"What's bugging him?" Bridger asked.

Tatum's soft reply never reached me. Probably for the best. She might be an excellent bassist and a beautiful woman, but I was still angry with her. I'd thought our talk after my mother's funeral had cleared the air, but she'd pulled her shit again onstage in London, and interest had sparked in her light hazel eyes again each time she looked my way. She wanted to fix me—heal me or some other stupid-as-fuck idea.

Reaching my dressing room, I snagged the bottle and tipped a long drag into my throat as I headed to the shower. I stripped down, kicking my boots into the corner, and stepped into the stall, ignoring the frigid spray as I took another pull on the bottle. After a moment, the water heated enough for me to wash the sweat and makeup from my skin. I set the bottle outside the stall and reached for my shampoo.

"So this is how you unwind?" Tatum asked. She opened the glass door, her pale, naked body gleaming under the harsh over-head lights. Her hazel eyes pleaded with me to love her. "I can help you with that. I'd be *happy* to help you." Her gaze dropped to my straining erection, part of every post-concert experience.

I didn't even bother to take it in hand any longer. I simply drank myself into limp dick. It solved lots of problems I didn't need. Kids were way up there—no way I was having kids and fucking them up like my parents did Lev and me.

"Get out." I shut my eyes and let the water cascade through the soap in my hair, trying desperately not to fall back into Aya's eyes from that night—that damn night that still gave me nightmares—or from the coffee shop, for that matter.

"I hate you."

She wasn't the only one. The more I considered the situation from Aya's point of view, the more I hated myself.

Tatum stepped into the shower behind me. Every muscle in my body went rigid as she ran her hands down my chest. I grabbed them before they dipped below my waist.

"I said get out."

"I thought we could shower together. Save water."

I bit back the words that floated across my tongue. *Can't you fucking listen? Are you stupid?*

That was something Brad would say. I wouldn't hurt Tatum the way he'd decimated me.

"I don't want you touching me. I don't want you in here, and I sure as fuck don't plan to share kisses or love words with you. I told you before—our relationship is professional, the band. That's *it*. And it's really, really starting to piss me off that you won't listen."

Her eyes took on a wounded sheen as she lifted her chin. Her eyeshadow and mascara ran down her cheeks, making her look like something out of a Stephen King novel.

"Fine. I'm leaving."

I kept my back to her, tense, until she stepped away.

"Who broke you, Nash?" she asked, voice soft.

"None of your fucking business. Now, if you don't get out of my shower and my dressing room in the next five seconds, I'm firing you."

"You can't do that," she yipped. "You need me."

"I need people who respect my boundaries."

Tatum fumed, but she stepped out. "She did a number on you," she tossed over her shoulder.

I grabbed whiskey and slammed the glass door shut. "No. I did a number on *her*," I muttered. I stood under the spray and swallowed most of the bottle.

Waking up in that hotel room, not knowing what day it was or where I was freaked me out. Not because it was abnormal—it had been my modus operandi for Steve to have to get me to bed for a while now—but because of who was in the room with me.

Lindsay. She sat on the edge of the bed, her hip near my foot.

I recoiled, nausea building in my throat. She stared at me, a strange gleam in her eye. I leaned forward and vomited much of what I'd consumed the night prior.

Never again.

That was the one thought rolling through my mind over and over as I spewed.

She shrieked, no doubt rousing everyone in the vicinity. Soon there were footsteps pounding outside the door. It flew open, and there stood Steve.

I glared at him, hating him more in that moment than I'd hated anyone. "I never want to see you again."

His face remained impassive as he nodded. "Before or after I get rid of her?"

"So this *is* your way of getting even? You let her in here." My throat felt raw as my stomach rolled again. "*Her*," I breathed as I retched.

"I let her in," Steve said, calm.

"I need to talk to you," she said, eyes imploring me. "I won't stay long."

I stayed sitting up, though everything in me wanted to flop back down and close my eyes. "Then say it so you can leave. *Jesus.* I can't stand looking at you."

She drew herself up, and I ignored her quivering lower lip. "Your precious Aya is getting serious with Alistair Seymour."

I raised my eyes to hers, all the hate I felt rushing back. "She isn't *mine*. She hasn't been since you drugged me years ago and made sure to humiliate her and ruin my life. Anything else?"

She fidgeted, seeming uncertain for the first time. "You can't let the situation between them continue," she blurted.

My brain might've been fried or scrambled or both, but even I could make out the pain in her features, the tension in her body.

"You care about this guy—this Alistair."

She pursed her lips, but she tipped her head up and met my gaze. "I do."

"Then I guess you're starting to know how it feels to have someone not give enough of a shit to step in. Oh, wait. You *did* step in. You fucked everything up."

Though I roared the last words, she stood firm before me, her gaze resolute. "I deserve that. Every bit. Look, Nash, I'm not here because I want to be."

I turned away, my throat working. My stomach threatened to heave again.

"Aya still cares about you. Her eyes never stop moving. She's been doing it for years, and she spends every soiree, every party, searching. Searching for you."

I laughed, but it cut off just before a sob burst from my throat. "That's where you're wrong, Lindsay. She hates me. Told me so herself."

Lindsay shook her head, eyes gleaming. "I don't believe it. You're wrong."

I took in her silk dress and expensive heels. Her hair was smooth and shiny, falling just past her shoulders. But her eyes were desperate. It was the first time I'd seen anything other than calculation in her gaze. For a moment, I connected with her fear and pain, but then I pulled back, remembering that Lindsay was a large part of the reason for my situation.

"What you want is for me to save a doomed love affair. Sorry to break it to you, sweetheart, but you can't save those." I pushed off the bed, shaky from my late night and the amount of booze I'd consumed during my shower ritual. I bit back a groan as I shuffled toward the bathroom. Everything hurt, with my eyes and my chest aching the most. Why was everyone so damn intent on bringing Aya back into my life?

Over four years had passed since Hugh's party. Four years since I'd lost her.

"Get her out of here." I thrust my thumb at Steve. "You, too."

Never again would I drink so much that I blacked out, I vowed. Never again would I look at Lindsay's face. Never, never again would I touch so much as a glass of liquor.

I headed for the bathroom.

My life was shit. I'd turned it to shit, just like my mother. I had wealth, I had fame, I had talent. But soon, I'd have none of those—at least if I followed my parents' playbook.

Brad was so broke, he was doing a reality TV show in Brazil. And my mother had sequestered herself away from the world in Pop Syad's mausoleum in Paris until her death. I had only visited her once because neither of us could handle more time together than that. The ghosts and recriminations between us had loomed too large. At least on my end. Her death hadn't changed that.

I struggled to align the toothpaste to my toothbrush before I raised my gaze and stared at my bloodshot eyes, my haggard face in the mirror.

"You're a fucking mess, Nash," I breathed at the man I didn't recognize. "Christ. You probably let Lindsay touch you. How would you know? You don't even know how you got to bed last night."

I shook my head, repulsion rippling over me. I brushed my teeth. After that, I stripped out of my boxers and got into the shower.

Cold water slammed over me, pelting my brain, but I stood there, jaw as tense as my body. Each drop hurt, yet I welcomed the sensations. For what seemed like the first time since Aya had breathed out those words, I *felt*.

It was horrible.

The water warmed and cascaded over me. I turned around and shoved my face into the now-scalding spray.

I was a mess.

I leaned over and retched into the drain one last time.

That was it—I'd reached the absolute bottom.

This couldn't stand.

I needed help.

I got out of the shower and wrapped my still overly sensitized skin in the robe. My head ached, and I desperately wanted a drink.

I ignored the urge and tried to stay focused, knowing I wouldn't last too long against it.

I walked out into the living space of the suite where Rod, my second-in-command, jumped from the couch. He seemed nervous.

Well, he should be.

"Where's Steve?" I asked. My throat ached. I closed my eyes, hoping I hadn't destroyed my voice.

"I don't know. You told us to get rid of him."

I nodded. *Right.* I had.

Except…part of me wanted the comfort of a friend. No, what I wanted was for Steve to step up and be the father I needed, but he'd never done that. Wouldn't or couldn't didn't change the outcome. I was alone.

"And Lindsay?" I asked.

"She's gone, sir."

I nodded. "Make sure it stays that way."

I needed to find my phone. I pawed through the sheets, my nose wrinkling at the smell from the soiled bedding. Eventually

I found it in the pile of clothes I'd worn yesterday, still on the bathroom floor. My legs were shaky, so I slid down to the tile. It was heated, warm, comforting.

I was supposed to do another show tonight.

I had a fully-booked schedule for the next three months. I'd kept myself too busy to think. Or rather, I'd tried to. Because even drunk or high, I could remember. I could wish for something different.

I leaned my head back and closed my eyes. Once I regained control, I dialed Cam's number.

"You know a place I can go?" I asked at his gruff hello. "A place that'll make sure to dry me out completely? I don't want to do this again." I laid my forehead against my raised knees. "I don't know if I can do it again."

"You're in Vegas?" Cam asked.

"Yeah."

"I'll set it up. Can you make it a couple of hours?" he asked.

I closed my eyes and considered his question. "Do I have a choice?"

"You've always had a choice, Nash. Just sometimes they're absolute shit options."

I chuckled, which caused my headache to grow. I winced, wishing I could grab a beer, something to take away the shakes.

But that's what had led me to waking up with Lindsay in my room.

Disgust forced me to lift my head. I gritted my jaw, determination overlaying the growing desire for a drink—any drink.

"I'll manage."

Chapter 9
Nash

After Cam had arrived to collect me at the hotel, we'd taken a short flight to Montana. Psychiatric and rehab facilities always seemed to be out in the middle of nowhere—probably so crazy-ass, entitled celebrities like me had nowhere to run and no way to get our fan fix.

Chuck settled in the driver's seat of our rental car at the airport, and my eyes ached too much to focus. Usually I bounced back by now, but this hangover had lingered. My entire body felt…off. I squinted as I lifted my sunglasses.

Cam settled into the back seat next to me.

"How's your wife?" I asked.

Cam had called a few weeks back to let me know Jenna was pregnant. That thought had rattled me, but Cam had been over the moon, so I'd decided to be happy for them both.

His smile widened. "She's good now that the morning sickness has passed. She's on a business trip."

"Oh? Handing off one of her guitars?"

"That was part of it. Now, she and Katie Rose—er, Kate are sightseeing in London."

London. Aya. It had been a month since our angry exchange in the coffee shop. We hadn't even managed a real conversation. Did she still live there, or had she come in for the show? I knew she'd graduated from Imperial College because I'd checked. But there was so much I didn't know. Had she gotten the job she wanted? Was she building amazing creations?

"You know, I spoke to Steve after you called," Cam said, pulling me out of my thoughts. "He said you gave him the boot."

I met Cam's gaze. "Needed to happen. He didn't protect me."

Not as a child from Brad, and not last night—today, whatever—from Lindsay. He was a shit father figure and a shittier bodyguard.

"He told me he wished, more than anything, that he'd handled the situation with Aya, when you were in the hospital, differently," Cam said.

I didn't have the energy to fight thinking about Aya any longer. She was everywhere, no matter how hard I tried. My longing for her slid out of the tight case I normally kept it in.

"I loved her so much," I said, eyes still closed.

"I know," Cam said with the quiet understanding of the guy who'd helped to pick me up the pieces after the fallout.

"Never told her that, though, did I?" I huffed out a dry laugh. "That's the joke, man. Jax, Bridger, *everyone* keeps trying to push other women on me, but I'll never want another woman like I want Aya. And I can't have her because I hurt her, the one thing I never wanted to do. That I cannot believe I *did* do."

That's why for so long I'd refused to see my actions through her reality. Now I hurt, too—for what I'd done *and* what I'd lost. No, Aya shouldn't blame me for being drugged, but how could she not question my commitment to her when I'd never actually made one?

When the car eased to a stop a while later, Cam turned to look at me. "I guess this is good luck."

"I'm going to hate it here," I muttered.

He nodded. "Yeah, you are. It's a military-style program interspersed with therapy. Steve told me about it."

"If that's the case, the next few weeks or whatever are *really* going to suck," Chuck chimed in.

"You're a dick," I said.

"Got a proposition for you," Cam said. He squirmed a little and squinted at Chuck, who nodded encouragingly in the rearview mirror.

"If you get clean and *stay* clean, Chuck and I will find you a new manager and head of security."

"Manager?" I asked.

Cam tucked his chin into his chest. "*He's* the one who let Lindsay into your suite."

My stomach flipped, even as impotent rage coursed through me. "Steve said he did it. Why would he do that?"

"He said you needed a wake-up call, and Lindsay was the best one possible."

"Not really an answer." But I hadn't the energy to process more information at the moment. "I need to take charge of my life, and that means of my actions," I told him. Cam had been the big brother I needed, the mentor who'd helped me find my place in the music world, and the friend I'd let down many times in the past few years. "And I'm sorry for not doing so sooner."

Cam scrubbed his palm along his jaw. "I had a bum deal growing up. I get some of what you went through. But I'd be lying if I said I wasn't pretty pissed with how you've squandered your time."

My throat tightened, and I dropped my head, unable to bear his disappointment. "There were a lot of days I didn't care if I made it to the next one."

He remained silent. I wasn't sure I breathed. Finally, when the silence became ponderous, I forced myself to look up.

"I know exactly how that feels," Cam said. He took my hand between both of his and squeezed. "And it would have hurt Chuck here, and my family, and me if you had managed to overdose or drink yourself into that oblivion you sought. So I'm glad you didn't. And you won't."

I shrugged. "I'm fixing me for me. I'm selfish like that."

Cam smiled, but it was sad. "You're the least selfish person I know. You're also one of the most sensitive. I think one of the worst things I ever did was let Asher offer you that recording contract. You weren't ready."

"I wanted it, though."

"Do you still? Knowing what you had to give up?"

I squinted at the large clapboard building in front of me. *Did I want it?*

Cam's tone became brisk. "Becoming a father puts a lot of things in perspective. I'm not going to be traveling as much. I want my kid to have no doubt who's the most important person in my life."

His gaze flicked to me, and though he didn't say it, I understood his message: I was the product of famous, wealthy parents. I was also on the road, forced to be "on" pretty much twenty-four-seven. Which made the drugs and booze seem like necessities to get through the grueling days. He didn't want his child to come in contact with the temptations he'd led me toward, no matter how unwittingly. I'd lapped all that shit up. I couldn't blame him for worrying.

"Maybe I'll pull a Shania Twain and make another record in fifteen years," he said with a smile. "Maybe I won't. I just know that now's not my time. Jenna and the baby, they're what matter."

I raised an eyebrow. "Sure wish my parents had thought that way."

His gaze remained steady. "I never told you why Carter and I didn't talk for years. I thought he had an affair with my wife."

"Jenna?" I gasped, the shock of such a suggestion rolling through me like wildfire. *Fuck.* I didn't know Jenna as well as I wanted to, but I'd been so sure she and Cam were perfect together. If I couldn't trust Cam's relationship with Jenna, then I'd been right to think love was fake, a manipulation.

Cam laughed. "Nah. Jen's as solid as they come. In love, anyway." His soft smile remained indulgent. But it faded. "I told you 'all in good time' about my first wife. It's time. She was into drugs."

Shame rolled over me, and I wanted to drop my gaze. I used all my willpower to keep my eyes on his.

He nodded, a rueful smile curving his lips. "She wasn't strong—or brave—like you, son. She was broken, emotionally, which is part of what drew me to her." He rubbed the back of his neck, sheepish. "I guess I'll always have a hero complex."

I snorted. "You sure did want to save me."

Cam put his hand on my shoulder and pulled me closer. I didn't like people to touch me. Ever since that model in San Francisco, I'd been weird about personal space. But this felt…safe. Right. I soaked in the warmth of his hand on my skin, the feel of being wanted enough, cared for.

Tears formed in my eyes. *Must be the damn hangover. I'm falling apart.*

"You're going to get well."

I cleared my throat of emotion. "I'd better go in."

"Think about my offer."

"Will do."

Chuck opened my door, and once I'd stepped out, he pulled me in for a bear hug. "I'll see you on the other side."

Chapter 10
Aya

I straightened my spine, which had the benefit of better showing off my cleavage in my midnight-blue Monique Lhuillier embroidered gown. I had to admit I looked stunning. My long, thick, dark hair was pulled up in a sleek, sophisticated twist, and I wore the most fantastic blue pumps with peacock-blue accents that matched the rich embroidery of my gown.

Unfortunately, I didn't much care.

Even the sumptuous 8 Northumberland Avenue's Grand Room, right on Trafalgar Square, was somewhat underwhelming. Ever since my last encounter with Nash—weeks ago now—I'd felt detached.

I focused my attention on the table where I sat, so far alone. The finest china and daintiest crystal settings were accented by fancy lotus flowers on the jade linen napkins and the low, but elaborate centerpiece of greenery, white lilies, and red berries.

I scanned the room, vaguely noting the crystal chandeliers and gilt trim, telling myself I sought Alistair, but the same restlessness I'd felt since seeing Nash reared up again.

"I hate you."

Why had I said that? I didn't hate him—not then, and pathetically, not now. I'd wanted so desperately for him to hold me, to tell me he was there, that no one would hurt me again.

"I hate you."

I closed my eyes against the harsh words. Against his shattered expression. Against the slew of articles I'd devoured recently that gave me the smallest insight into Nash's life. There was little to work with. Pictures of him mourning his grandfather, head bent, had crushed me. He'd looked so alone, so lost.

But still, I hadn't called.

"I hate you."

I knew Nash created songs both for himself and other performers. He toured almost constantly. He'd just bought a house in Austin's Barton Creek neighborhood. He remained estranged from his father, Brad. Recently, more stories had emerged citing his erratic behavior. He'd recently fired his long-time head of security, Steve Lincoln.

A pretty blonde slid into the green velvet seat next to me at the table set for six. "You must be Aya." She smiled as she arranged her voluminous, cherry red, satin gown, which undulated to the floor. "I recognized you from photos, though they don't do you justice. I'm Jenna Grace."

"I am. A pleasure. Do I know you?"

"I'm Camden Grace's wife," she said, her tone cheery but her eyes watchful.

"Oh." My pulse pounded against my neck. "Congratulations."

"Thanks. We've been married long enough now that I don't get those much anymore." She smiled again. "You look *just* like the picture Nash keeps on his nightstand."

My tongue felt heavy in my mouth, like it wouldn't unglue enough to let all the raging thoughts in my head pour out.

Probably for the best because I wasn't sure what this woman wanted from me.

"Mama Grace speaks fondly of you," she continued.

I smiled at my memories of Camden's mother: soft hands, gentle voice. Crispy fried chicken and sweet tea that slid down my throat with refreshing coolness on a hot summer day. She'd been kind but preferred the background. She'd smiled down at her pies as Cam and Chuck needled each other or Cam and Nash jammed on their guitars.

"She's lovely," I offered.

"She said she's starting to feel her age." Jenna shook her head. "I think it's to guilt us into having more kids." She patted her belly. "But I'm not sure I can handle more than one, especially if it's a little hellraiser like Cam." Affection laced her words. She blinked up at me, all innocence. "Was Nash mischievous?"

My upper lip stiffened, but I managed to say, "I don't want to talk about Nash."

"Didn't figure you would." Jenna shifted her weight. "Anyway, being pregnant is wreaking havoc on my insides. You'd think a bean couldn't do so much damage, but it's bouncing around worse than a bad mosh pitter." Her eyes glowed with happiness as she placed her hand on the small bump there. She leaned in close. "I wasn't sure I wanted Cam."

I blinked, trying to keep track of her ping-ponging topics. "Okay."

"He's intense. A lot to handle."

"O-kay."

"And he's been hurt. Deeply." She shook her head. "Not unlike Nash. He's a mess, you know."

I raised my eyebrows, ignoring my clammy palms. "Cam?"

"Well, Cam, too. But he's gotten so much better since he made peace with his past. He and Carter are close again, which helps immensely." Jenna studied me. "Cam called Nash the night after he saw you at the coffee shop. I don't think Nash remembers, though. He drank himself into a stupor."

I clenched my hands into fists, but kept my mouth shut.

"He never reached out again, did he?" Jenna sighed. "So that's why you don't know…"

I bit the inside of my cheek, trying to calm my racing pulse, suppress my need to ask. Jenna could continue to play whatever game she wanted, but finally, after all these years, I was moving past Nash's rejection, his betrayal, and the pettiness of high schoolers. Progress, I supposed. Though I didn't feel much better for it.

I refused to close my eyes, knowing the image of Nash on the stairs—swaying, screaming at me, his eyes hot and angry—was there. *Just there,* if I let it out.

And the avalanche of hurt that came with it would bury me, yet again.

I hated how easily I fell back into those shame-filled memories. Hadn't I just said I was making progress? Clearly not.

The image of Nash clasping Lindsay's hand, of her walking him up the stairs to the *sex palace,* as the other teens had deemed any bedroom in any of our houses, caused a fresh slice through my pounding heart. The shame and embarrassment never left.

In some ways, it was even more a part of me than the grief I felt surrounding my mother's death.

"I was hurt like that—like you were—once," Jenna said. "Around the same age as you, too. I needed a year away from those kids to find my footing enough to move forward."

She knew. Of course she did. Anyone could find the video from that night. No doubt it was *still* plastered all over the Holyoke crowd's social media, still there for people to see—to laugh at. Humiliation rolled over me again, each wave larger and more painful than the last.

While Jenna seemed nice, and certainly chatty, I refused to relive those dark moments from high school again—particularly not here at The Children's Gala. It had been years. I was a different person. A stronger person. I had a degree, a career I loved.

I gathered my clutch and began to rise, unwilling to continue this conversation.

"Since you've taken Alistair's seat, I'll move over." I rose, turning away.

"Is that your boyfriend?"

I hesitated. Alistair and I dated. We called each other for social engagements. "Yes."

"The stuffy dude in the tux over there?" Jenna tipped her head. "The guy who was just telling his bros how he'd let you work for a year, maybe two, before you transitioned into your 'proper place' as the lady of the house?" Jenna's lip curled. "Like it's the Victorian era and our uteruses make it impossible for us to use our brains."

"Alistair said…" I shook my head. No way he'd talk about

me like that. What else had he mentioned? My hands tingled, icy cold, at the mere thought of him mentioning personal details of our relationship to his friends. He wouldn't…would he? "You must be mistaken."

Jenna shrugged. "There's a crew of frat boys over there." She waved her hand, and I noted Alistair's dark hair among them. "Seems like the douches here just speak with a better accent."

My eyes widened. "Your comments are uncalled for. I'd appreciate it if you'd leave me alone."

She sighed, eyes downcast. "Sorry. I guess you do like the guy."

I paused before I managed a smile. "Cam was always kind to me. Please give him my regards." I said nothing about her, still unsure how I felt about this woman who insisted on blindsiding me with my past.

A niggling concern spread as I considered her comments about Alistair from my new seat. He'd asked me to attend this event with him, saying he wanted his family to see me as a capable hostess.

Because he thought I'd give up my career and do this full time?

"Steve said Nash was high and out of his mind at that party back in Austin when you finished high school," Jenna continued, leaning over to bridge the space I'd just put between us, "that some Lindsay chick drugged him. That's why he didn't come right after you. After that, from what I understand, he was hurt. Deeply."

I flinched as I did every time someone mentioned him. And that happened with more frequency since he'd hit the pinnacle of music success. While his songs tore up the charts, Nash's smile had become more vacant, his cheeks hollowed out. His eyes had been glassy that day at the coffee shop. Since then, I'd read all sorts of rumors about his use of drugs and alcohol. Was that when it had all started? With Lindsay?

"*She* drugged him?" I couldn't stop the catch in my voice. He'd acted so out of character that night…more aggressive, angrier. Scarier. Had none of that been his choice?

Regardless, he hadn't been the man I'd loved—the man I needed to hold me, to grieve with me. He'd *smashed* me to bits that night.

Jenna tipped her head, a frown creasing her brow. "Hugh said he told you."

I fidgeted as emotions swirled through me. "Hugh told me Nash was hospitalized. I was a mess because my mother had just died so… I don't know. I never realized Lindsay drugged him…" I trailed off.

I'd broken my rule—I didn't discuss Nash. I didn't discuss my time in Austin. That's how I'd managed to survive.

I licked my lips as I strove to calm the jitters racing over my skin. "I think I could have liked you," I said. "Goodbye."

Jenna rose, her eyes sad. "I could have liked you, too, but I'm pretty angry that you're willing to throw Nash away for a frat bro."

"You have absolutely no right to judge my choices," I snapped, finally losing my cool.

Jenna's small smile turned brittle. "I have more right than pretty much anyone else. I've *lived* that shame, your current fear. You don't like what I'm saying because I'm hitting the raw spot."

I turned away, my jaw clenched. But angry as I was, I couldn't make myself leave. I wanted to—and also I didn't. Jenna could provide me with more information about Nash, and I craved that knowledge like a junkie seeking her next hit.

"He's in rehab," she informed my back, as I continued to stand near the table.

I quashed the stirrings of sympathy and cut off Jenna's careful words and cautious tone. If I didn't, I'd fall back into the loop of wanting Nash, only to be blanketed in shame. He'd hurt me so deeply, and I… I looked away, my stomach tightening.

I'd hurt him back that day, in the coffee shop. I'd cut him just as he'd cut me.

The difference was, his hurt remained private, between the two of us, whereas mine was still watched by people on the internet.

"He seems determined to destroy himself," I finally told her, turning back around. "After the childhood he had, no one can blame him. And the money, the fame, all the perks of celebrity status just make it worse."

He'd commented on it when we were kids. No one felt sorry for the rich kids. He'd never really stood a chance at normalcy, let alone at receiving sympathy and help.

Jenna smoothed the silk of her skirt as she rose. "Nash gave this to Cam after he saw you at the coffee shop and asked him to make sure you received it."

She held out a small box. With shaking hands, I took it.

"Why didn't Cam give it to me?" I asked.

Jenna raised her eyebrows. "I asked him the same thing. He said why should he?"

I bit my lip, tears pressing at my eyes. I'd cut him out of my life—simply carved Cam and his family away the same as I had Nash.

I lifted my gaze to hers. "Nash shattered me," I whispered.

Jenna's eyes softened and she moved closer, almost as if she wanted to hug me. "Only the people we truly love have that kind of power. And for the record, he's never recovered from the part he played in hurting you."

My lip quivered and tears clung to my lashes. Jenna reached out and squeezed my hand. "I wouldn't be here if the situation wasn't dire." She met my gaze. "I really hope you're the woman Cam thought you'd become. The one Nash needs now."

Chapter 11
Nash

The rehab facility reminded me of a rugged Western lodge—a mix of river stone and heavy timber, but with upscale fabrics and finishes. The food was an appropriate mix of fresh produce, most of it grown on the surrounding land or in greenhouses, and lean protein. I'd eaten more fish in the past three months than in all the rest of my life together. While delicious and filling, I missed pizza. And steak. But I was surprised at how few cravings I'd had for chips and sodas. If nothing else, I felt cured of the worst of my junk-food fetish.

In fact, for the first time probably ever, my body felt healthy. Not necessarily strong—not yet—but on the mend toward wellness.

Health was a strange concept, because any one answer could produce either a positive or negative reaction. One drink relaxed me, but I never stopped at one. And the drugs I'd taken—progressively harder and stronger shit in an effort to forget my mistakes, my hurts—had created a ripple effect that destroyed my ability to sleep, winding the spiral for destruction tighter.

But when I was in the murky shadows of addiction, I couldn't *see* these obvious details—at least according to my new sponsor/ therapist/life coach/enforcer, Jordan. The *enforcer* part was my least favorite. Currently, the tank of a man had me sweating and heaving my way through what I hoped were the last fifty burpees of my life.

"Getting better, kid," Jordan said. His brown eyes sparkled with pride then humor when I collapsed to the floor, my arms shaking too much to lift myself even once more.

"When do I get out of here?" I gasped.

"After your shower," he said.

"Not the gym. *Here*. This facility. I've been here ten weeks."

"Eleven as of yesterday, which is about two weeks sooner than most people leave. You're doing great, though. I think you're almost there. You've worked hard, and that shows."

He reached down and grasped my hand, his larger one engulfing mine, and pulled me to my feet. My legs trembled after the hour-long workout, but they held me. I was stronger, steadier, just as Jordan had promised.

And I'd learned that I'd turned to booze and pills because they dulled my emotional responses. I was still rocked by the realization that I was a sensitive soul. It's probably why I'd been drawn to Aya in the first place, but it was also why I hadn't been able to handle her leaving—and why I hadn't been honest about my feelings for her.

"Are you ready to talk to Steve?" Jordan asked.

I scowled. "No."

"You're going to have to deal with him, what he represents both in your past and your present."

"I'm aware. But I'm not ready to do that yet."

He clapped me on the shoulder, and dread pooled in my gut.

"He's here, isn't he?'

Jordan nodded, causing his brown waves to flop onto his forehead. "And if you want me to clear you to leave, you'll talk to him."

I scowled as my gaze drifted toward the door. "Are you going to let me shower before you force me out there?"

Jordan chuckled. "Nope. Best to rip the Band-Aid off."

"What if I'm still bleeding underneath?"

Jordan's eyes filled with compassion. "That's exactly why you need to do this now."

He walked over to the door to our private gym, his white sneakers squeaking across the wood floor. He opened it, and a blast of trepidation hit me right in the solar plexus. My hands shook as I stared across the room at Steve.

He'd aged—or maybe I was simply noticing him, *seeing* him for the first time in a long while. I studied the gray threaded through his sandy hair, the crow's feet around his eyes from squinting. His eyes were a darker brown than mine and looked back at me with as much concern as I felt welling up in my gut.

"Hi," he said. He took a hesitant step into the room. "You look…"

"Not plastered?" I offered.

He nodded. "You look good."

I scoffed. "I'm scrawny and gaunt. I'd scare a kid if I walked past one."

His smile slipped from his lips as quickly as it came. "Maybe."

Jordan stepped out of the room.

Steve took another few steps forward, his hands clenching and unclenching at his sides. "Look, Nash, I'm sorry."

"For?" I asked, eyebrows raised.

"A lot of things. But I'm not sorry I let Lindsay into your room. She was the wake-up call you needed."

"Cam said that was my manager."

Steve swallowed. "No. That's on me. I don't like your manager because he supplies your drugs."

I shook my head. "So you had me fire him."

"Yeah. I knew thinking he'd let Lindsay in would be reason enough."

"It was."

I turned to stare into the wall of mirrors, my thin face staring back. I'd lost the sallow skin and dark-ringed eyes that proclaimed poor health. My cheeks glowed pink from my recent workout, and the muscles in my shoulders and arms were sleek, tight. Yesterday, Jordan and I had looked at the headshot taken when I entered the facility. I liked this version of me much better.

"I'm not sorry for that either," I said. "I was on a bad trajectory. He needed to go."

"You were. Had been, and I didn't know how to stop it." He took another couple of steps. We were maybe ten feet from each other now.

I inhaled. "I'm still very angry with you."

He dipped his head. "You should be. I fucked up."

"When did you start to wonder?" I asked.

Steve cleared his throat. "You're nothing like Brad."

"For which I'm very thankful. So why didn't you find out?"

I cocked my head to the side and waited. He rubbed one of his palms across the back of his neck. "I had a shitty childhood."

"Welcome to the club," I muttered.

"No, I mean *shitty*."

I glared at him. "Like your parents ignoring you after your brother died? Or how about your mom skipping town rather than being around you *ever*? Your dad calling you stupid and worthless? Or worse, he's not your dad, and the hired help shows up and says, 'Hey, I could be your dad—don't know, don't care, because I didn't want you in the first place'? That must be what you mean when you say shitty. Because if you mean your dad hit you, I'd take that over the neglect and psychological bullshit I've been forced to live with since you showed up."

Steve cleared his throat. His eyes were misty, full of old memories and something that looked like…fear. As if he believed I would reject him. "He did hit me. Often. He beat my mother into such a pulp, she died."

I closed my eyes and inhaled sharply. "Yeah, that's shitty," I managed to choke out. "And now I owe you an apology. I'm sorry."

He edged closer, and his hand found my shoulder. "I know I failed you. Hell, everyone in your life who was supposed to protect you failed you. Except Cam and his family."

"And Aya," I said. I blinked my eyes open, shock causing my mouth to gape. I hadn't meant to say that, to even think it. But her name spilled out.

Steve nodded. "She was the best thing that happened to you."

I raised my eyebrow. "I thought you'd say that was Cam introducing me to Asher Smith."

Steve shook his head, face serious. "If I could go back and kick my own ass, I would. I was star-struck and excited for you to take that deal. Hell, I told your mom you wanted it, glossed over all the stuff Asher and Cam said about maybe you should wait. They were right, you know. Taking that contract then? It wasn't the best choice for you."

The weight of this conversation made my chest ache. I lowered myself onto the bench-press bench. "It wasn't the best choice for Aya and me. She knew it, too. She knew it even though she supported me."

Steve knelt in front of me, his palm on my cheek, his fingers on my neck. His eyes were murky. "As I said, not the best thing for *you*."

I bit my lower lip. His touch stirred emotions in me, ones I hadn't felt in a long time. Good ones—safety and love. I wanted to shrug him off, but even more I wanted him to draw me into his arms and rock me like my mother used to.

A sob bubbled up my throat. I shoved it back down. "Are you my biological father?" I asked.

He dropped his hand to his knee, and his lips compressed into a thin line. He looked into my eyes. "Yes."

I exhaled, but it wasn't a harsh breath of recrimination. It felt cleansing. "Okay."

Chapter 12
Aya

"I really don't need this," I muttered as I hung up the phone, annoyance spiking through me. Alistair had demanded that I meet him in an hour at a posh London restaurant.

My hands shook, and I bumped the small package Camden Grace's wife had handed me off the counter. I hadn't had the courage to open it, nor had I found the will to chuck it, so it had sat there, on my kitchen counter, for weeks. Taunting me.

On a held breath, I studied the now partially opened cardboard gift box. A note peeked out the side. Definitely Nash's handwriting. I scooped it all up and set it on the counter next to my purse. I moved to the other side of the kitchen, turning on the kettle to make a cup of tea. The package tugged me back toward it.

But I had no time to open it now. I brushed my hands over the silk of my dress, eliminating any tiny wrinkles. We were good together, Alistair and I. "*A perfect match*," my father had said.

Much as I liked Alistair, I couldn't escape the fact that I'd gone out with him that first time to get even with Lindsay. That sat poorly with me. I hated realizing I'd become the very type of woman I'd always despised: a woman like Lindsay.

Tension built in my neck at the mere thought of my father. He'd manipulated me for years. That realization hurt as well, but

I had to face it if I was going to have a chance to overcome it.

He'd manipulated me into paying for his lifestyle—using the very money my mother and grandfather never wanted him to have.

I shivered.

But at the same time, even if my father wanted me with Alistair for all the wrong reasons, I did like him. He was the first man to make me laugh, to listen to me and show interest in my pursuits since…

My gaze went back to the package as I lifted the kettle. I winced as a few drops of boiling water splashed onto my fingers. I set the kettle down and rushed my hand under cold tap water, gritting my teeth against the burgeoning sting.

That's what Nash did—he caused pain. First emotional and now physical. I shut off the water and dried my hands. I picked up the package and marched to the trash bin.

The writing on the side caught my attention again, just as it had each time I'd planned to bin it. *Please don't throw this away. Please, Ay.*

And, much smaller, so small that I had to basically press my nose to the paper to read the tiny, messy cursive: *Not like I threw away the best thing that ever happened to me. (That's you.) And please believe me when I tell you I was yelling at Lindsay, not you. I swear this on Lev's grave.*

I gulped. Nothing was more important to Nash than his brother. Maybe me, for a time, but Lev had been his best friend as well as the big brother he'd looked up to. I dropped the box back on the counter, my eyes burning and fingers throbbing.

"You bastard. I was finally moving on. Finally! It's taken

years…" I closed my eyes and tipped my head back, trying to find some peace. But meditation no longer came as easily as it had when I'd lived in Tibet. Or even in Austin, where I'd felt grounded and safe, thanks to my mother and Nash.

I attacked the box, clawing at it. I had to know what he'd sent me.

I broke three of my nails in the process and winced at the blood oozing from one of my cuticles as I fumbled to open the pretty wooden box inside. It looked like it had been carved in Tibet. I frowned. When would Nash have traveled there? *Why…*

My breath caught and tears spilled over my lashes as I stared down at the malas. I gasped as their cool weight settled in my palm, which warmed the beads. These weren't the ones that had broken that day in the coffee shop. A pang filled me. *Dammit.* I missed those beads—that connection to my mother. But Nash and I had broken that string. We'd severed their connection to each other—just as I'd hoped we'd sever ours.

That's why I'd told him I hated him.

I touched the jade beads. Jade represented the heart chakra, loving energy, and healing.

"What are you playing at, Nash?"

I'd expected *my* malas. The ones my mother gave me. I set the beads back in the box and slammed the lid shut. I swiped at my tears, huffing out a big breath in an attempt to get myself under control.

I headed down the hallway to my bathroom to wash my face, angry with the redness around my eyes. I reapplied basic makeup with hurried strokes and then had to change my dress and shoes after I bandaged my fingers, which had left smear marks all over the pretty fabric.

I refused to look at the package as I collected my purse and coat. I marched to the door and even made it halfway out before I turned back and grabbed the box, stuffing it into my bag.

I locked the door and headed off to brunch, though my mind kept circling back to Nash's laughing eyes and sweet smile.

Chapter 13
Aya

Alistair met me just inside the door of the restaurant with social kisses on each cheek. He swiped raindrops from my shoulder as I handed my umbrella to one of the staff and noted my bandaged fingers with concern—after he'd squeezed them and caused me to wince.

"What happened?" he asked. His brow puckered.

"An incident with the tea kettle," I replied. "The worst part was I didn't get my cup."

"We'll rectify that now, darling." He seemed to hesitate. "Since you're improperly caffeinated, I'll tell you your family and mine are joining us today."

I jerked back, nearly bumping into another patron as they entered. My purse slid down my arm and plopped to the floor, disgorging the contents.

I gritted my teeth in frustration as I bent down to gather everything. I had been fine until Jenna had handed me Nash's package. Now I was a mess of nerves, and I didn't like the live-wire feeling.

"Damn him," I murmured.

"What was that?" Alistair asked. He rose to his feet in a graceful move, the Tibetan box in his hand. I reached for it, but he already had it open.

"What extraordinary craftsmanship. Are these from your mother?"

I chewed on the inside of my lip. "My mother gave me a set years ago," I said, opting for diplomacy.

"Ah, right. They're lovely. You should wear them. You know, to showcase your heritage."

I hated how easily Alistair conflated East Asian customs with my mother's background. I wanted to snatch the box away and tuck Nash's gift out of sight—and out of mind—but once again, Alistair was a step ahead of me. He pulled the bracelet from its velvet lining and settled it around my wrist. The tassel tickled the delicate skin there, making me even more aware of the connection with Nash I would never be able to break.

Sure, we might be continents apart, but Nash knew what these beads represented and where they came from. And he'd chosen this stone to indicate a message, one I wasn't sure I wanted to acknowledge.

Still, I couldn't help but touch the intricate carvings on the small beads.

"Lovely." Alistair beamed. "Now you're an elegant mix of East and West." He plopped the box into my purse and scanned the space.

I frowned at his comment, mulling it over in my mind. A bracelet didn't change my appearance or integral beliefs. To think that was shallow. Vapid, even. Or... I swallowed back my sudden concern that Alistair was so unaware of the rest of the world that he simply assumed such comments were benign and not judgmental.

But that couldn't be—Alistair was considerate. Even now, he settled his palm at the small of my back and guided me toward our table. The more cynical part of me wondered if he worried I'd bolt and wanted to be able to catch me before I darted away. Not telling me he'd invited my father… I touched the jade beads, letting them steady me just as the set my mother had given me had. I'd missed that connection to her terribly.

Nash, by giving me this bracelet, had managed to give me back a piece of my mother.

I drew in a long, slow breath that filled my belly from the bottom up and released it just as slowly. I could handle my father's machinations, Alistair's, too. I could also handle my continued unabated infatuation with Nash Porter. I'd survived my teenage years and was beginning to thrive, finding my niche professionally at an electric-vehicle company owned by one of my father's colleagues. While I'd originally wanted to go into aeronautical engineering—work for Virgin or Elon Musk's space company—I'd created a life for myself, possibly with some affection and a partnership with Alistair.

We needed a few more months, maybe a year, to work through the kinks, for me to be sure he understood my goals for myself, how important it was for me to honor my mother's family…

"Surprise!"

I jolted back to reality, my shoulders tensing at the smiling sea of faces. My father's grin was wide, his eyes warm as he offered me benign acceptance. His wife, Lady Harriet, gave me a tight-lipped smile—the closest to a look of approval I'd ever received from her.

Alistair's parents clapped politely, seeming a bit less enthusiastic about the affair. I could completely understand.

"What…" My voice trailed off as my gaze landed on the chilled champagne bottles and the banner hanging that read, *Congratulations, Alistair and Aya.* Below our names were entwined rings.

"Were you not planning to discuss marriage with me before you announced it?" I whispered, swaying slightly.

Alistair shifted on his feet, his gaze drifting to my father's. "Why would I want to minimize the surprise? This is romantic—a whirlwind of romance."

Alistair seemed to be parroting words, the words my mother had told me my father said when he'd asked her to marry him. Why on Earth would he have thought they'd be what I wanted to hear?

My skin seemed to tighten. I didn't want this. My gaze continued to roam the assembly of faces, seeking something.

Then my eyes stopped. *Lindsay* stood off to the side, seemingly out of place. She was pale, her eyes even more red-rimmed than mine from my earlier crying jag. She didn't try to smile. She downed the mimosa in her hand and grabbed another. A heavyset older gent stood next to her, his jowls quivering in indignation as he glared down at her.

That must be Lindsay's father. I'd never met the man and didn't plan to. He lowered his head and grumbled something, causing Lindsay to flinch, her face going slack with…was that fear?

Despite everything, sympathy stirred in my gut. Lindsay cared deeply for Alistair—even more than she feared her father. Those emotions clashed together for her today. Her father strode off, no doubt having told her to behave or else.

I knew a bully when I saw one. I studied Lindsay, noted the longing in her eyes as she gazed at Alistair, which reminded me of how I must have looked at Nash. And, just as obvious, Lindsay cared enough for him to show up at his engagement to another woman. She was unhappy but putting on a brave face—something I'd never done, I realized.

I'd never given Nash the opportunity to explain, and I'd never been willing to examine why things might have happened the way they did at Hugh's birthday party. I'd just assumed, carried off on a wave of hurt and fear and insecurity. Lindsay had been pretty, the most popular girl in our school. I'd always felt dowdy and less-than next to her, so when I saw Nash wrapped around her, I'd accepted that as truth, rolled over without a fight. I'd been too ashamed, too grief-stricken to process any of it or stick up for myself, for what I'd had with Nash.

Instead I'd run. I'd let my father take my phone. I'd let Harriet soothe me, telling me I didn't need those terrible *children* in my life—that they wouldn't benefit my new station as the viscount's oldest daughter.

I hadn't fought. I'd accepted. Existed. That's all I'd done since.

My breath hitched, and I smoothed the malas. What would my mother say to this set of events? To the way I'd allowed the world to dictate its terms to me? I rubbed my opposite thumb over the beads, letting them settle me. My breathing evened.

Alistair had assumed I'd marry him because he was an earl. He was such the catch in London circles that he needn't ask me because *of course* I'd want him. He clutched my waist, reinforcing the idea that he planned to keep me nearby. The light in Lindsay's eyes dimmed further as she grabbed another glass.

Sweat slicked from my armpits and down my back as I realized Alistair was just like my father: a manipulative man who'd force a woman to bend to his will, her opinions and feelings notwithstanding. I knew in that moment that what Jenna Grace had told me she'd heard him say at the bar at The Children's Ball was one-hundred-percent true.

My head began to ache, and I let the bracelet's tassel feather over my palm. I couldn't believe how much I'd missed its soothing weight, this feathery touch. Only now was I finally whole, finally able to see clearly again.

I met my father's gaze, time seeming to slow. If I refused this, he wouldn't simply be *disappointed* in me. It would mean losing my position at his friend's firm. However, though I liked the work, I wasn't sure I cared. Additionally, I'd be free of my father's monthly financial needs and all the reasons he asked me to just help a little more, a little longer, to let him and Harriet give my sisters "*the lives they deserved, after all.*"

If I withdrew my financial support, he'd ban me from his home. When and *if* we spoke, the conversation would likely be limited to the same series of unflattering comments about my life, my clothes, my choices.

If we spoke.

But thanks to Alistair, we ran in the same circles. *Currently.*

My gaze settled once more on Lindsay, who, surprisingly, met my gaze. Heartache seeped from her eyes, reminding me of how I'd felt when she tugged Nash up the stairs. She must have been remembering too, because her eyes filled with tears and she looked at the floor. After all this time, had Lindsay *finally* realized how much she'd hurt me? I could certainly return the favor. In fact, part of me wanted to, just so Lindsay would comprehend fully what it meant to have her life's dreams utterly crushed.

She looked up and licked her lips. Tears spilled down her cheeks as she mouthed *please*.

The quiver of indignation swelled in my chest.

"Well?" my father said, impatience seeping into his tone.

Alistair's hand tightened at my waist, and at least fifty sets of eyes were glued on me.

"Such a lovely couple," I heard Lady Seymour murmur.

"They'll be the new Meghan and Harry," someone added.

"Alistair says her foreign blood will strengthen our Eastern fiscal ties," Alistair's father said. His voice carried a bit, and the underlying concern permeated both his expression and tone. "But I hope she's ready to start a family, give up that career nonsense and give us grandbabies. A woman needs her place."

I stiffened, affronted by his words. "I'm a person, you know," I said, keeping my voice low, expression neutral. "And I don't intend to quit working."

"Father's pompous," Alistair said with a charming smile. "He means well but can't understand why I'd be head-over-heels in love with you when I could have chosen a sweet English girl."

My gaze slid back to Lindsay. Even she, half American, would be preferred as a Seymour bride. So what had made Alistair seek me out? My stomach sunk as if I'd swallowed lead.

"A nice English girl who planned to pop out kids?" I asked. "When would you tell me I couldn't work any longer? A year? Two, if you felt generous?"

"Why would you want to work?" Alistair asked. "You have enough money to—"

And there it was. The real reason he'd sprung this brunch on me. He planned to use my money and force me out of my career—just as Jenna had said.

I clenched my fists, grounded by the throb of my burned fingers. "How much did my father offer you?"

Alistair blinked. His mouth tightened but he turned me gently, cupping my shoulder blades. "Is your self-confidence so terrible that you cannot believe I love you?" he murmured. But his blue eyes were calculating behind that soft expression.

"I'm assuming the amount is substantial," I continued. "Did he tell you about my trust fund, or did you already know about it when you sought me out at that party last year?"

Alistair's lips tightened. "This is vulgar, Aya. We're at our engagement party."

I touched the bracelet once more before straightening my spine. "You never asked me to marry. And for the record, the money is all in a trust that requires my signature as well as my solicitor's, *not* Lord Aldringham's. He cannot touch the money, nor can he offer it to you. I bet he failed to mention that. Just as he failed to mention that I don't get access to more than half of the money without further stipulations."

Stipulations I hadn't bothered to read.

I'd rectify that, soon.

No more allowing others to dictate to me. No more hiding behind old hurts, the humiliation and shame of my past. *No more.*

My mother's smiling face flashed into my mind. "*You are worth so much more than you give yourself credit for, mon mignon,*" she used to whisper. No, I was worth exactly what I allowed myself to be worth. And I needed to show my father what that meant.

As Alistair paled and cut a scathing glance toward my father, I knew I'd guessed correctly. He cared more about my money than me.

"If you'd bothered to ask, I would have explained my financial situation to you," I told him. "And now, because you tried to force me, the answer is definitely no."

I spun on my heel and threaded my way out of the restaurant, clutching that stupid tassel as if it were a talisman.

Chapter 14
Aya

I stepped out onto the street, back straight, chin up, and my legs trembling. I assessed the row of gleaming vehicles at the curb and a distant double-decker bus as my heart continued to race like maracas.

Returning to my flat didn't seem smart. My father would show up and rage. Still, I had to leave this area before Alistair tried to talk me into his way of thinking.

I'd gone along with it before, not caring enough, but… Jenna's comments continued to flit through my head. And the malas, *my malas*, I decided, had ignited some tiny spark inside me. Now a flame had flickered to life. I didn't wish to be the foreign bride of a British aristocrat as my mother had been.

I clutched my handbag to my chest, feeling a little lightheaded. What a bloody awful time to realize my blunders. Rain dripped down my face and into my eyes. Not a taxi in sight. I turned left and began to walk, in three-inch heels not made for traversing distances. I pulled out my phone, hoping to find a rideshare vehicle nearby that could take me to a hotel where I could regroup.

"Need a lift?"

I turned toward the street to find Lindsay in the back of a charming, mid-century Aston Martin painted a sparkling black, its chrome shined to gleaming. I hesitated.

"I know you don't trust me, and I understand why, but please, let me do this for you. Alistair's recovered from the shock and your father…" Lindsay grimaced. "He's the biggest asshole I've ever met. And that's saying something, because I grew up with a terrible asshole."

My lips twitched. Lindsay opened the door, and after another second's hesitation, I slid into the luxurious interior. I looked up, shock reverberating through my body as Lindsay gripped my burned, torn fingers.

"Thank you. I know you didn't tell Alistair no for me, and I know I don't deserve anything from you, but still…thank you."

"You love him," I said, shaking my head. I hadn't thought Lindsay capable of real feeling.

She laughed as she blinked back tears. "Since I was seven. Isn't that ridiculous? And yes, I know that makes me an even bigger dick for crushing on Nash and being willing to take him to bed all those years ago. You need to know we never slept together—I never touched Nash again after Hugh's party, because he didn't want me to."

I remained quiet, processing. I'd ended up in a vehicle with Lindsay Herrington-Smythe, my teenage nemesis.

As if she could read my thoughts, she said, "High school was a destructive time for me. My parents' divorce had upended my life. Alistair and I had always been close, and suddenly, I wasn't able to see him. I was furious and devastated. I had sex with boys I didn't care about and who didn't care about me. I lashed out at you. At everyone, really." She dropped her gaze. "It's not an excuse. I know I was wrong. And so mean. When I learned

Alistair was interested in you, I assumed it was my penance, but seeing you two together…"

Her lower lip wobbled as she raised her gaze. "I love him, and losing him devastated me. But even saying that doesn't encompass what you and Nash had. If I hadn't been so selfish, so willing to make others hurt just because I did, I would have realized that."

I extricated my aching fingers and gave my hand a shake.

Lindsay zeroed in on the bracelet. She narrowed her eyes, but then gave a tiny nod. "Did you know Nash went straight from Vegas to a three-month rehabilitation program?" she asked.

My stomach clenched. "I heard. From Cam Grace's wife. She was at The Children's Ball."

"Mmm. I was there—in Vegas."

I narrowed my eyes. "Do I want to know?"

Her smile turned rueful. "Nash hates me more than you ever could." She hesitated but then clamped her lips shut and shook her head.

"Tell me the rest," I said.

She raised an eyebrow at my tone. "Steve asked me to visit. I hoped Nash would come after you, sweep you off your feet—"

"And you'd collect Alistair," I finished.

She shrugged. "That would have been ideal."

I clutched my purse in my lap. "Where are we going?"

"Do you have your passport?"

"I do," I said. I never left my flat without it—another way to ensure independence from my father.

Lindsay leaned in, her blue eyes wide with a fire that used to mean she planned to rip some poor girl's self-esteem to tatters.

But this seemed more tempered. Maybe I was searching for humanity where there was none. Or maybe Lindsay meant what she'd said.

I couldn't be sure.

"What's left for you here, Aya?" she asked. There was a softness to her voice I'd never heard before. "Do you even like England?"

No, I don't. This place had never felt like home. The last home I'd had was Austin—not just because of my relationship with Nash, but its small-town charm and big-city amenities. The place was flush with STEM jobs and ideas. The lakes and bike trails begged to be used, and the summers were hot and sunny— perfect for outdoor activities, unlike the constant gray drizzle I'd survived here.

But that wasn't the point. I missed Austin, but my life was here.

Wasn't it? Did I even have a life?

Lindsay *was* tempting me. I narrowed my eyes. "Ah. With me gone, you plan to have Alistair marry you—for your inheritance. I guess that means he's the clichéd impoverished nobleman seeking an heiress."

Lindsay tossed her head, the proud, obnoxious girl I'd known back in full force. "That is my plan, yes. One my father wants with more desperation than I do—the one thing we have in common. For the record, I didn't care about Alistair's financials until he passed me over. But yes, I'll still marry him. Once I get him to ask me. I do think he cared for you, so his wounds are going to smart."

I raised an eyebrow. "His pride, you mean."

She smiled, a wide, genuine one that caused her eyes to

sparkle. "Oh, you trampled that, and I, for one, enjoyed the show. I expect his mother to start the smear campaign on your reputation and good works by the end of the day."

Lindsay reached forward but dropped her hands before she touched me. "I'm sorry," she said. "Really. I picked on you because you were different. You never seemed to fit with us, and Nash never cared."

He hadn't. I was the one who'd been insecure.

"Nash gave you that bracelet, didn't he?" Lindsay waved her hand. "Don't bother answering." She pulled out a piece of lined notebook paper and offered it to me. "This is Nash's address." She dropped her gaze. "Hopefully the program worked, and Nash is once again in control of his faculties."

My pulse sped up. "Why do you have that?"

She hesitated but once again shook her head. "Steve gave it to me."

"*Steve?*"

Lindsay sighed. "I told you: he called and asked if I'd come to Vegas. He said Nash needed a push, and I was the best person for that job, seeing as how I'm the one who started the chain reaction." She pinched her lips together. "As much as I hate being the villain in your story, I am, and I'm sorry."

I studied her, searching for deception. "I'm not sure I believe you."

She shook her head. "Look, here's what you have always failed to grasp about Nash Porter. He's one of the world's most eligible bachelors. He's gorgeous, and he's *never* been interested in a woman who isn't *you*. Most of us can't stand that. At least

I couldn't—drove me crazy that he never even looked at me. I came up with all kinds of dreadful reasons why destroying your relationship was nearly as good as having him for myself."

I mulled that over. "Okay, but why would you help me?"

"Fair question. But am I really helping you? I mean, you know I want Alistair."

"I think you *are* helping me, and it's making me uncomfortable."

Lindsay stared at me for a long moment. "Maybe I'm not the complete ogre you thought I was. Maybe I've learned some things about myself and the world. Or maybe it could be a wild goose chase, and I'll enjoy laughing at your expense. Ah. We're here."

She opened the door and ushered me out into the watery late morning. Then without another word and only the smallest of waves, she shut the door and her car pulled from the curb.

I turned to face Heathrow Airport.

My phone buzzed, and I pulled it out, unsurprised to find a voicemail from my father. As dread settled its heavy weight over me, I pressed the play button and stared up at the terminal. Over the drone of jets, my father's sharp voice filled my ears.

"Aya, if you do not return to this restaurant in the next fifteen minutes, I will disown you. I'll tie up your money in the courts, and I will personally see to it that you're sacked."

No, I never really had liked England. Maybe it was time to go home.

I clicked off my phone and walked into the airport.

Chapter 15
Nash

Why had I thought being home would help me get past the restlessness that continued to itch my skin? Including my time in rehab, I was one hundred and one days sober now, and I'd celebrated earlier today at the Grace family ranch with a large slab of Mama Grace's peach pie.

Surrounding myself with loved ones had helped to temporarily mitigate the itchy feeling, but I'd had to pretend not to see the side-eyes filled with concern. Each time Cam, Jenna, Kate, Rye, Steve, or Mama looked at me, I'd felt the weight of their worry, the heft of their hope.

"How's it going, son?" Steve asked, poking his head around the wall that separated the kitchen and dining room from the expansive living room in my Austin home.

I shivered, as I did each time he called me that, because the meaning had entirely changed. Like the word, the relationship needed time to settle on my skin and sink in.

"It's not."

"Want to watch some TV?"

"No."

"Need a snack?"

He'd taken to treating me like a toddler. I frowned but didn't bother to lift my head from the couch cushion. "I'm good. But thanks."

"Well…"

"I'll call you if I need you."

"Yes, sure. Of course."

Awkward—just like every other interaction we'd had over the past couple of weeks. But we were talking, even if our interactions didn't exactly rise to the level of conversation. Mainly, I suspected Steve checked in on me to ensure I was sober.

I was, and I definitely planned to stay that way, but contentment flitted beyond my reach. I sat up and finished my glass of sparkling water. No way did I want to slide back into the oblivion, though. Even if this place hurt.

I stared up at the coved ceiling. Not a speck of creativity had flowed through me since I got sober, no matter how long I held my guitar—a gift from Jenna and one of the finest works of craftsmanship I'd laid eyes on.

Oh, I had songs in my head. Beck's "Loser" was the loudest, and Radiohead's "Creep" settled in for its say, too. But no new melody twined between them, pushing those back.

I'd felt like this since I gave up the substances—though, honestly, I hadn't produced much that wasn't crap in the year before I went to rehab. I'd been disconnected from everything. But whatever the reason, I hated my inability to make *something*. I'd held on to the belief that I would find my muse again, but now, months after I'd admitted myself and a month since my return to life, I just felt…empty.

It was a terrible feeling.

Not that my loneliness was new. Those two songs had taken

up residence years before and rarely left for long. And beneath them, Patsy Cline twanged out "Crazy." I was crazy because I couldn't get over the most recent society photos from the *Sunday Times* early edition.

It was one of my only clues into Aya's life, and I tortured myself with the possibility of seeing her face—and who would be next to her. She'd been linked to multiple men since she'd left Austin, all of whom I wanted to punch in the face.

Much too often these days, Lord Dipshit and Aya were together. I lifted my head and stared at the image spread across my coffee table: Aya wearing a beautiful, peacock blue, embroidered gown, her lovely dark waves tamed into a rich-lady updo reminiscent of my mother's. And her hand on Lord Dipshit's arm. I'd glared first at the photo, my shoulders relaxing a fraction when I noted the lack of a ring. But the article was three months old, as was the photo. I was still catching up on British society news—well, information about Aya. I'd flung the paper down after I'd read that "sources close to Lord Aldringham expect an engagement announcement between his eldest daughter and Lord Seymour shortly. The ensuing union would tie together two powerful families in Britain."

I closed my eyes. Aya marrying a lordly prick to appease her father—I never would have believed it.

That's what she'd become. I thought I knew her better than that. I'd been so sure she'd see through the social climbing and...what?

Come back to me?

That had always been my fantasy. But it wasn't as if I'd made any move to tell her I still wanted her—no, *craved* her. I craved Aya Aldringham with more of a hunger than I'd ever had for the pills or powders I doused myself in.

Not that it mattered.

"I'm heading out, son," Steve called.

He rounded the corner and spread his arms. "How do I look?"

His hair had grown out, meaning he needed product to tame the wavy mass. His eyes were sharp and hard under his thick, brown brows. His cheeks were sleek and cleanshaven, and his dark blue button-down was tucked into a nice pair of khakis—with a *belt*. He wore shit kickers, which kept me from completely hating on his outfit.

I rose from the couch and swiped at the newspaper.

"You look good. Shirt's a good color."

The fuck I knew about fashion, but I did like the shirt. Steve filled it out well, and he was in better shape than me. He called it *fifties fit*, whatever that meant. He was mean about workouts when I didn't fall into line with his daily torture, so I did my damnedest to stay on his good side.

"Enjoy your night," I said.

I heard his boots cross the hardwood as he moved into the kitchen ahead of me.

He stopped at the back door and cursed. "Are you expecting someone? Do I need to stick around? You could have told me. I got a hot date, and Sherry is not going to like me standing her up."

I stretched, trying to work the kinks out of my shoulders. "Nope. I'm not expecting anyone. You know that, seeing as only you and the Graces even know I'm back in town."

That probably wasn't accurate. The media must know I was home by now, and the paps all wanted their shots of Nash Porter, post-rehab.

I wasn't in the mood for company. Already Steve was on my nerves just by being excited about a date. The uncaring asshole. He knew I was in a mopey stage.

"Well, a car just pulled onto your road. I expect them at the gate…"

The chime blared, and Steve scowled.

I strode past him into the kitchen alcove—what used to be the butler's pantry—where I kept one of the monitors. I looked down into the face that stared back and gripped the edge of the counter as my knees buckled.

Unfortunately, my fingers slipped, too, thanks to the bloom of sweat that exploded on my palms and at the small of my back, temples, and upper lip. I landed hard on my ass. The air rushed out of my lungs, and my vision tunneled. At least the damn songs faded behind the ringing in my ears.

"Nash?" Steve's severe features appeared in front of my face. Concern morphed into trepidation as he studied me. If I looked half as bad as I felt—pale, shaky, sweaty—then I was a total mess.

"You with me, son?"

"Aya," I whispered.

"Whoa. You sure?" Steve turned toward the monitor.

My ass ached nearly as much as my lungs. I couldn't draw a full breath. My vision still seemed narrowed. "I told you, I—"

"Are you going to let her in?" Steve asked, cutting me off. "Because she's starting to look like she regrets pressing the button."

I rose to my feet so fast my head seemed to float away from my body, and I pressed the gate release so hard I jammed my knuckle. I was a mess.

Sure, I'd been thinking about Ay—I *always* thought about her. But I wasn't prepared to see her, talk to her...grovel at her feet. Not now, not when I was so recent from detox. Not when I was still trying to figure out how to be a real person.

Why was she here?

"Marry Me" by Thomas Rhett spilled through my head, followed by Lewis Capaldi's "Before You Go."

That second tune suited Aya and me better. I wanted to touch her.

I wanted to taste her mouth.

I just wanted to hold her, soaking in her scent, the softness of her hair and the warmth of her body.

Maybe, for the first time in years, I'd feel like I was home again.

Why was she here? She had to hate me. She'd told me she did.

"Get out of here," I told Steve, making a waving motion with my arms.

"Knocked you flat on your ass," he mumbled. Then he clapped me on the shoulder. "Are you okay with this, son?"

I shook him off. I'd showered recently, but I was wearing old jeans and a years-old T-shirt that had become a favorite simply because I'd had it so long. The logo was mostly faded to nothing, but it was soft, nearly threadbare in places. I looked...not my best. Not that I'd looked or felt that way in ages.

I'd wanted to dazzle Aya if I was going to see her again. I

stared down at my bare feet. This outfit definitely wasn't going to do it. I barely looked like I could dress myself.

"Nash? I'm worried about you."

Right. Steve. I tried to remember what he'd said.

"You and me both. And my guess is I'm going to need you around to keep me sober when she leaves. So, enjoy your few hours or whatever with the Sherry chick."

Steve muttered a curse. "There goes my only chance at sex."

"Well, at least you *have* a chance at it."

Steve narrowed his eyes. "I keep telling you, it's not healthy to repress—"

"Not interested," I shot back.

The monitor now showed Aya approaching the circular drive out front. "And your opinion doesn't matter because I'm about to get my balls handed to me."

Chapter 16
Aya

Nash Porter, the world's sexiest man, as well as one of the hundred richest, opened the door to his house himself. His eyes widened, almost as if he couldn't believe what—or rather who—he was seeing.

His hair was longer, brushing his collar and drifting over his ears, and faintly damp from a recent shower or swim. His T-shirt clung to his chest, making it clear that he still worked out with the gusto he had back in high school.

Always lean, he was now broader in the shoulders and thicker through the arms. His features were still classically handsome, notable in their symmetry, much as his mother's had been, but they were both more defined and more rugged, as if he'd lived hard.

From what I'd read, he had.

A hint of shadow dusted his jawline, sharpening it. His lashes were long, and his eyes were still wide, the ever-present storms raging through their brown depths. I used to stare at Nash when he wasn't looking, trying to decide if his eyes were more light brown or tawny. I'd never made a decision, but today they seemed to radiate deep emotion, which tugged at me with just as much potency as the dazzling spirals of color dancing toward his pupils.

His jeans were soft and old, giving me a great view of his

thighs. He tugged at his shirt, seeming concerned it wasn't pulled down fully.

I froze, my stomach hollowing out as I wondered if I'd caught him right after a tryst. My gaze darted over his shoulder, waiting for a lovely young woman to stroll out into the room. Half-naked, probably. Definitely freshly fucked.

I slid my damp palms along my rumpled skirt as surreptitiously as possible, hoping to wipe away the shame.

Of course Nash had a woman here. Why wouldn't he? He was Nash Porter, most recent winner of the world's sexiest smile.

Yes, that was a thing. I'd stumbled across it on the Internet because I'd wanted to know what he was up to—and who he was dating. The Internet claimed he'd bedded every beautiful woman, yet none seemed to stick around for more than the one article linking them together.

"Aya."

My name from his lips sent emotions cascading through me, my gaze darting back up to clash with his. Goose bumps rose over my arms in a ripple of awareness, much like I suspected I'd feel if a lightning bolt struck close by.

He waited, no doubt for me to say hello. But I had a more burning concern. "Did I—am I interrupting something?"

"No, and if you were, I'd get rid of whoever was here."

I plumbed his eyes, seeking truth in his statement. He reached forward as if to grasp my wrist, but he must have changed his mind because he let his hand fall. It hit his thigh with a soft thud, causing me to jump.

I'd spent all of the thirteen-plus-hour plane ride, layover in

Dallas, and the final leg of the journey to Austin's much smaller airport fluctuating back and forth over what to say to him when I arrived.

I touched the tassel of the malas. Nash's gaze dipped to them, his expression frozen, as if he were holding himself back.

Did he want…? He seemed to want to touch me.

I wanted that, too. Except I didn't. I couldn't. Nash and I were strangers.

Weren't we?

"I saw Lindsay," I managed to choke out. I cringed. As if that information was most relevant. Well, it was part of the catalyst for my being here, so I guess it was.

"Will you come inside?" he asked.

I gripped my purse strap and hovered at the threshold. Finally, after an agonizing moment, I crossed into Nash's home.

It was large—I'd known that from the sprawling facade. But I hadn't expected it to be so…homey. His parents' house had been a showstopper, designed to awe guests with their taste and wealth. Everything had been oversized and sleek. I'd always considered their house like a castle—until my father had moved me into his family home. Its original structure, around which the manor had been built, had been a keep. Then I'd realized how much nicer the Porters' home was, and less drafty.

Nash's home seemed comfortable and lived in, with lots of hardwood and earth tones. A round, low-slung wooden coffee table sat between two couches. On it rested an empty glass and a notebook with a fountain pen atop it. A gleaming guitar leaned against the couch.

"Were you composing music?" I asked.

"Yes." He rubbed his palm over the back of his neck, dropping his gaze. "Well, I was trying."

"Not a good session?"

He shot me a look from under those thick brows. Some would claim it was a smolder, but I knew this was just Nash—always intense, driven, yet off balance by my presence, unsure what to do with me.

That made two of us.

"Do you really want to talk about my songwriting?"

I shook my head. With effort, I slid my purse from my shoulder and settled it behind the nearest couch—not the one Nash clearly preferred. It wasn't leather but a micro suede. I ran my hand over the soft, tan material.

Nash followed, close enough that I could have touched him as he skirted around me and settled on the love seat across the coffee table. He placed his guitar back in its case.

Space it was, then. I swallowed down the nausea and butterflies. I'd expected nerves, but this level of anxiety surprised me. Yet behind the fear of him rejecting me *again*, a faint hum settled. The rightness of being near Nash, of being in his space, soothed something in my chest.

Perhaps I was finally done looking for him, as Lindsay had accused me. Or done standing on the sidelines.

I managed to settle my butt on the edge of the sofa and folded my hands in my lap, atop my pressed-tight knees, ankles tucked to the left.

"You look good," I ventured. His tee showed off his strong

arms and defined chest. I refocused on his hair before bringing my gaze back to his eyes.

Nash tilted his head, much like a predator trying to get a bead on its prey when it hadn't simply run away. "So do you. Ravishing, in fact."

I patted my hair even as I scoffed. "Sixteen hours of travel are never kind, Nash."

"Sixteen? Ah. Commercial. You are so like your mom." He smiled.

It was brief, but it was filled with nostalgia and humor, and it stole my breath.

"Why are you here?" he asked. "Not that I'm not glad to see you," he rushed on. "I am." A faint blush bloomed across his cheeks. "I couldn't believe it when you pulled up to the gate. I thought this had to be a trick for a pap to get inside."

Right to the point, then. A bowling ball seemed to lodge against my windpipe. "No trick. I saw Lindsay."

"You mentioned that."

"She…ah…helped me."

"Really?" He looked uncertain, the storms building in his eyes.

"We hadn't spoken since…" I huffed. "Since the night I saw you going with her up the stairs." I forced my gaze to meet his, stay there.

A deep furrow built between his brows. "Not in all this time? Don't you run in the same circles?"

"I refused to acknowledge her."

A smile flitted across his lips. "That's ice cold."

"She didn't deserve my friendship," I snapped.

He shook his head. "No, she didn't. She was never kind to you, which was most of the reason I couldn't stand her."

He took in a long, slow breath. I noted the fine blades of his cheekbones, the faint pallor under his normal skin tone. He wasn't at death's door, as Lindsay and even Jenna had suggested, but he'd been unwell recently.

I opened my mouth, closed it. Time rushed past, even as it seemed to slow down. I had no idea how long we sat there. Nash's chest rose and fell in shallow bursts. His nostrils flared, and his face grew more menacing. He was beautiful. Not in a Michelangelo's cold, marble *David* way, but as a perfect specimen of masculinity. Nash was warm. His lips were full and a little too pink, and his cheekbones, thanks to that illness, were better chiseled than David's.

"I needed to see you," I finally told him.

His breath stuttered, but he remained silent.

I clenched my hands into fists and pressed my thighs together. *Get the words out, Aya.*

"I…I was offered an engagement."

His gaze shuttered, his face leeching of that animation I'd been admiring as well as all color. "I see."

"I declined because…" I squeezed my legs even tighter and straightened my spine. "Dammit, Nash. All it took was Jenna Grace bringing you up, and I couldn't let this...*thing* between us fester any longer. It's been years. I've been angry, hurt, humiliated. I need to hear what you have to say so I can let it go. Let us go."

"Is that what you want?" His voice was raspy. The muscles in his face shifted, turned hard. "If so, there's really nothing to say."

I slammed my teeth together so quickly I winced. "I think there is," I managed. "You never told me *why*."

He rose in one smooth motion, a caged tiger on the prowl. "You disappeared before I could."

I scoffed. "Like I was going to stick around for you to fuck Lindsay mere hours after you'd left my bed."

He flinched so hard he stumbled. He rested his hands on the back of the nearest sofa, his fingers gripping to the point his nailbeds turned white.

"For the record, I *never* touched her—not on purpose, anyway. She drugged me. I was trying to get away." His eyes sought mine, storms raging. "I wouldn't have done that to you, not even high on meth and LSD."

"I thought… The other students were already deriding me. My mum had just died—"

He pressed his fingertips to his eyes. "Shit, Aya, that was a bad night. Don't you think I go over it in my head? Wish I'd never gone to Hugh's party? Never gone home to see why Brad was texting me? If I'd stayed at your place, you would have curled up next to me, tucked in close. We could have cried together, been in shock together."

"But we didn't. You hurt me," I said. My jaw quivered. "No, you publicly humiliated me right at the time I needed you most…" I shook my head and rose on unsteady legs. This wasn't how I'd wanted this to go, but I couldn't help myself. The sleepless nights and jet lag seemed to catch up with me in a rush, and I swayed. "I guess that's that. History aired."

I forced myself to turn my back and round the sofa, keeping

my dignity intact. The next move was Nash's. I collected my bag and headed toward the door.

Nash stepped in front of me. His palms slid around my shoulders, bringing my body closer to his. I wanted to lean into him, to rest my head on his shoulder to have him hold me as he used to. To hold me like I needed him to.

That's why I'd come here. I might've professed that I wanted to clear the air for my return to Austin, but really, I needed *him*, the only person in my life I'd relied on besides my mother. I needed Nash to offer me the comfort he hadn't that night.

I tipped my head back, lips parted to ask him what the hell he was doing.

His eyes were filled with remorse. "I'm so sorry about your mom, Ay. I'm so, so sorry I wasn't there for you."

He held me loosely, giving me the chance to break away. The silence stretched, spiraled. I waited.

"I know how the video looked. And I'm utterly sorry I hurt you—especially then, when you needed me."

My breath caught, and tears built in my eyes. "I…" I whispered. "I gave in to my fears. That's why I didn't give you a chance to explain. I was sure you wanted Lindsay because all the boys did." I dropped my head. "I was wrong—for believing you wanted her, but more for not having faith in you."

Nash studied me a moment. "I just got out of rehab," he said.

I supposed he thought he was admitting some great sin. Or some great secret.

"I expect you and the rest of the world know that," he continued before I could respond. "One of the things I did at that place, something new, was therapy. I spent hours in it—first to figure out what's wrong with me and then to work on how to fix it."

I frowned, unsure what this had to do with me.

"When Lev died, my parents basically abandoned me, Aya. Until you showed up—at first just in emails and texts—I had no one. I never felt safe. Then, I wrapped myself so tightly around you that I didn't let you breathe. I didn't let you be whoever you needed, wanted to be. And I didn't know what to do when you pulled away. After I saw you with that first boyfriend, everything turned hopeless. Touring was exactly what everyone had told me it would be—a grind. I drank too much. Then I picked up pills—all the things I'd watched Mom do to ease her pain."

He shook his head. "Eventually I didn't remember *days* of my life, and that scared me. So I had to take a long look at my choices, what I'd done to myself. I've had to sit down with all the important people in my life and tell them how much they mean to me and how sorry I am for my choices and the pain they caused them."

He tugged me a little closer, his face shining with earnestness. "I've done a lot of that, but it's always been *you* I needed to apologize to the most. Because I loved you, Aya—even way back then. Even before I could figure out how to say it."

My eyes widened. Noting my reaction, he smiled, but it was tremulous—so un-Nash-like. Nash was bold, confident. This man seemed unsure, but filled with fortitude.

"I'm sorriest that I never told you that." He swallowed. "It's what sowed the doubt between us. I understand now how much you needed reassurance. But all I could see was how supposed *love* had caused my parents to destroy each other. And they dragged me down into their cesspit with them."

I hadn't much considered how his parents' messed-up marriage had impacted his ideas about love—that wasn't at all like what we'd shared. We'd been laughter and purity even when the world attempted to intrude. But his parents had circled each other, making sure they were photographed with a person the other hated, going to great lengths to goad and hurt the other through the media, who printed each scrap for fans to lap up. Because I hadn't realized that's what Nash thought of as *love*, I'd been hurt when he wouldn't tell me he loved me.

Yes, I'd been wrong, too. So very wrong.

No one, me included, had considered how those words, those images impacted Nash. I swallowed, realizing the disservice we'd all done to the young man searching for his way, longing for acceptance and connection.

He slid his palms across my shoulders and up the sides of my neck. He cupped my cheeks, his thumbs against my temples. "I couldn't articulate it back then because the only word I knew represented what had happened to my parents. I was too afraid of what that could mean for us. But I understand now that you've always been my person, my love, *my home*."

Chapter 17
Nash

Relief rushed through me. It felt so good to finally say that. My fingers eased off Aya's cheeks, and I smoothed my palms up and down the soft skin of her arms, worried I'd left bruises when I'd grabbed her. Caring for another—or myself—wasn't something I'd focused on in recent years. But inherently, I wanted Aya to be safe. Safe and happy. Preferably near me. Scratch that. *With* me, on me.

The opening refrain from Coldplay's "The Scientist" drifted through my head, the soft piano building to Chris Martin's melancholy lyrics. Beautiful as that song was, it was soon overwhelmed by Lewis Capaldi's "Before You Go." It still seemed to fit Aya's understanding of me then. I wasn't sure how to fix that. I rarely cared what people thought of me. I didn't need to. But Aya's opinion mattered.

I cleared my throat. These fucking emotions, the songs battering my brain, wreaked havoc with my ability to communicate, but I persevered. I had to. So much needed to be conveyed before she tried to bolt again.

Which I understood. Fuck, I understood Aya's need to hide away better than anyone. She had slid into numbness just as surely as I had downed liquor and pills to get to the same place.

"I've needed to say that to you for years," I told her. "I should have said *this* long before, too. I love you, Aya Jane Aldringham. I didn't say it before because of my fear of messing us up. Turns out *that* destroyed us, and I can't let it sit between us any longer. *I can't*, pretty girl."

She stared up at me, her eyes wide, guileless, burning into my deepest, darkest secrets. They were all about her, so really, she had every right to them.

She inhaled hard through her nose. "You're right. It *was* fear." She clasped my wrists, her fingers cool, her grip strong.

"I've never said 'I love you' to anyone since Lev, and I only said it to him when he was in a fucking coffin." I paused, considering my relationship with words. I wove stories with them, evoked emotion in others. Yet in my own case, three words had destroyed my world.

Her face softened, and her lips parted. "Oh." The sound escaped as if she couldn't hold it in any longer.

I brushed my knuckles over her cheek, trying to ignore the flurry of nerves blooming in my belly. "I wasn't ready for you. Not if I wasn't willing to admit my feelings for you. I see that now."

Her eyes closed, and a small pucker formed between her brows. *Good*. She was listening to me.

"When you disappeared, I pretended I didn't care because I knew if those little punks realized how much I needed you, they'd…" I pressed my lips closed. "That was my fear, residual from high school and courtesy of Lord Prescott, but it doesn't matter. What you need to know is I was hurting. I thought you'd broken your promise to me. By the time I realized… I hurt us both, Aya. I cut myself so deeply I needed years to find my footing. If nothing else, can you believe that?"

She remained still. After a long moment, she opened her eyes and studied me. Her gaze started at the top of my head and swept over my face—like one of those facial recognition scans—before returning to my eyes, holding them, searching. I held still, doing my best not to shut down. I desperately wanted to, though, because letting Aya in was the most vulnerable I think I'd ever been.

I thought I'd given her my heart that day I'd first talked to her about Lev, and in a way, I had. But I hadn't realized then how much trust I'd put in her, nor had I realized how careful she'd been with me. Not until I smashed us all to hell. But I was done being careful. I had to be. Now was the time for boldness, honesty, abandon.

"I'm glad you didn't drown… You're pretty."

That vacation, when I was five, maybe six. *That's* when I fell in love with Aya. My words had been simple but, she and I had clicked. And somehow, we'd reconnected in high school.

Regret swamped me, making my throat tight and achy.

Aya's nostrils flared, and her eyes seemed to beg me for… something.

"What, love?"

That endearment suited Aya and her place in my life as my top priority. I wanted to smile, but she was still skittish, obviously hurting. I pressed my mouth flat instead.

"I'm scared."

Her voice cracked, and my muscles tensed. I needed to soothe her.

"Of what?" I asked.

"You."

Chapter 18
Nash

Her lower lip trembled so much that her teeth clattered. She heaved a breath. "That you'll leave me."

Words tumbled out of her mouth, faster and faster, like rain spilling onto the eaves. "That you'll realize what I've always known: I'm shy, a bookworm interested in making things, and you're…you're changing the world. Even before things fell apart, I worried you'd break up with me once you realized I don't want to tour endlessly; that roots matter to me in a way they don't to you because I never had a permanent home."

She stayed still under my hands, but she wasn't passive. She was exerting her will in her own way—quietly, as Aya did most things. She let me touch her because she knew it grounded me in the moment, but when she'd said her piece, she would ease away. And if I hadn't convinced her by then, she would walk. Because Aya was strong, stronger than me. She had an inner will that kept her from collapsing under the weight of her emotions—most of the time. I envied that inner strength. I always had. It was one of the traits that drew me to her, that caused me to love her, however incompletely, all those years ago.

"If you break my heart, you'll still be here, in this world," she continued, her voice cracking. "But if you die… Jenna told me how close you were to overdosing. I can't live in a world without you, Nash. That would be so much worse." Her jaw trembled. "I'm not trying to force us to be together. I came back because I've missed Austin. It's the last place I was happy." She sucked in a harsh breath. "I wanted to come home."

I pressed my thumb to her lower lip, taking in her eyes, the slope of her cheek, her precious chin, those soft lips. I tried to speak, but had to clear the emotion from my throat. "I was happiest when you were here. I believe we could be happy again. I don't want you to be afraid." I sighed. "I need to tell you, I wasn't fair to you before."

Her breath caressed my finger as her brows tugged lower.

"Listen, I'm still learning as I go, but this is important. You were my foundation. My rock. Lev was dead, Brad was angry, and my mother was absent—she ran. Right when I needed her most."

Aya dropped her gaze, her face twisting. "You call him Brad now," she observed.

Ah, right. Another truth she didn't know. I hated that I had secrets from her. "Because he's not my father."

Her nose wrinkled. "Can't say that's sad news."

I chuckled. "Me neither. Some of the best ever. Just…the timing sucked."

She sighed. "That night?"

I nodded.

"It was a terrible one," she said.

I leaned in, pressing my forehead to hers. "I was caught in a situation I didn't fully understand, caught between adults who should have supported me but either couldn't or wouldn't. That goes for Steve, too."

"Steve?" she asked, brows tugged together in confusion.

"I'll get there. For now, I just need you to understand that I didn't plan to make you my lifeline, which, in turn, made me your anchor."

"That's not true," she burst out. "Why do you think I felt weighed down by you?"

"I think you *still* do," I told her. "You said it yourself: *we don't know what's going to happen*. None of us. I could die. So could you. Lev dove into the lake and never came out. But I promise you, I want to live. I want to be present. I won't try to destroy myself ever again. *Now* matters a fuck-ton, because we have it. We have a chance to make it what we want it to be. I don't want to squander that."

Her eyes widened, searching. Her need to feel secure, to feel loved, was palpable around us, melding with my same needs. But this time, Aya was asking *me* to be strong. That wasn't my typical role. I knew how to lock myself down, and how to drink and medicate myself into an uncaring state. But standing up, taking charge—not a position I was used to.

Nevertheless, I stood taller, squared my shoulders. For Aya, I'd do it. I'd be the man she craved, the man she *deserved*.

I hadn't been that before, and it had cost me years of my life that I'd never get back, never remember clearly. No way in hell was I going to let my fear, my weakness destroy more of either of our lives. We both deserved more.

"We have now, and right now, I can tell you that I love you. I've loved you for years, pretty girl."

She chuffed as she pressed her cheek more firmly into my

palm. Her eyes told me she'd felt our crazy connection from the beginning. We'd been changed by those early messages—both of us—and for the better, at least in my case. Amazing how the world could have spun a different way, but it didn't. And I had to wonder why.

I let the soft heat of her skin warm me, settle me.

"You saved me," I told her. "That's not hyperbole. I was drifting when I sent you that first message. Nothing mattered. But you... You gave me hope, a reason to keep striving. And when I let fear overwhelm me…" I swallowed, my teeth clenched. "After you left, I faded back to that thing I was before, and I hated myself because I'd lost you."

I steadied myself, kept my gaze locked on hers. "*I love you*, Aya."

I let those words linger. I wanted her to feel them, as I did.

"I love you with a passion I'll never have for anyone else. I couldn't; it's you I see. It's always been you, and it always will be."

I brushed her hair off her temple, a simple gesture of affection I'd made so many times before. But I'd lost the right for so long—to simply touch her. I smiled, even as the gravity of that settled over me. I thought again of all we'd lost. I rested my forehead against hers, my palm sliding down to capture her neck, tugging her even closer so our bodies touched from forehead to hips, all aligned. And it still wasn't enough.

"You're *literally* my other half. I need you. Not just want, or crave, or desire, or...or whatever. I *need* you, Aya Jane Aldringham. I'm not talking about grounding or calming me—I need to tell you my secrets, my fears… I need you in my life. Always."

I breathed out the last word.

She inhaled shakily, her eyes huge in her pale face. Tears wet her lashes. "With my mum, it was easy. We had a simple life in all the villages where we lived. I never had to struggle for a place, to understand the jockeying and backstabbing of this world. I'm not good at it. So I can't do this with you if I'm also freaking out about whether there will *be* an us. You say we're two halves of a whole. Well, when you run, when you hide behind others instead of staying, of talking, it chips away at me, and we can't…" Tears dripped down her cheeks. She needed another breath to go on. "We can't fit together. My heart can't fit yours." She shuddered with a great sob.

I wrapped my arms around her, determined to do this. "We have now, and tomorrow, and tomorrow, and tomorrow."

She huffed a laugh. "Are you going to tell me this is a tale spun by an idiot?"

I shook my head. "No, but I am glad you caught the *Macbeth* reference."

"Because I made you read it."

I smiled.

She closed her eyes and pressed her forehead more firmly to mine.

Her answer at this moment would change us.

For better or worse.

I hadn't realized the weight of that.

I was better with her. So much better. I could feel the weight of it creaking against my shoulders even now.

"I'll propose," I blurted. I dropped to my knee, pulled her to sit on my raised thigh. "We'll get married. We'll build our life, one that no one can rip apart."

She opened her eyes, the purple irises stark against the red-rimmed lids.

"You and I both lived through our parents' failed attempts at marriage," she said.

"We aren't our parents," I said, desperation churning my guts. "Hasn't that always been the point we've tried to prove? You're not a fusty British peer, and I'm not a man led by my dick." I winced.

This proposal was shit.

"You get what I'm saying. We're not our parents. We've lived through their train wrecks and know what that feels like. We won't get married without weighing the risks, but I know you're worth every single one."

She settled on my raised knee and wrapped her arms around my neck. She pressed her lips to mine. They were cool, soft, salty from her tears.

I wanted this kiss to spin out into forever. I wanted this to *be* my forever.

She pulled back, her eyes filled with the shadows I'd helped create. "Nash…"

I stared at her, my back slicked with sweat. But I waited. This had to be her choice. Even as much as I needed her, I knew I didn't deserve this opportunity. I was selfish and I'd begged, but I wouldn't force her.

She deserved more than that. She deserved…everything.

I hadn't given her everything, even now. I cupped her jaw,

tipped her chin, and kissed her. This time I didn't hold back my confusion or pain, the fierce love, the deep affection. I put it all into that kiss. She pressed back, and I tasted anger and betrayal on her tongue. I shifted, softening, letting my body tell her I was sorry, so damn sorry for my teenage stupidity, for hurting her so much.

She clasped her palms to my cheeks and accepted. She relaxed and let me make the same promises to her lips.

She pulled back. "I'm pretty sure I still love you, Nash. You know that. So I'll give you this chance to prove you mean it, but please." She moved all the way out of my arms, wrapping hers around herself. "*Please*. Don't hurt me. Don't hurt yourself."

She rose, and I caught a glimpse of hurt in her eyes. "And don't propose to me unless you know in your bones that you want to marry me—and you'll be faithful forever."